Burns und Lambert

Eva Fitzgerald

Scenes in Erin and the sister isle

Burns und Lambert

Eva Fitzgerald
Scenes in Erin and the sister isle

ISBN/EAN: 9783741194214

Manufactured in Europe, USA, Canada, Australia, Japa

Cover: Foto ©Andreas Hilbeck / pixelio.de

Manufactured and distributed by brebook publishing software
(www.brebook.com)

Burns und Lambert

Eva Fitzgerald

EVA FITZGERALD;

OR,

SCENES IN ERIN AND THE SISTER ISLE.

That soil full many a wringing despot saw,
Who worked his wantonness in form of law.—LARA.

LONDON:

BURNS & LAMBERT,

17 & 18 PORTMAN STREET, PORTMAN SQUARE,
AND PATERNOSTER ROW.

1861.

To the Long Suffering and Noble-Hearted Catholics
of Ireland,

This humble little Work,

founded on recent events, and yet but very feebly
illustrating the many wrongs they are
called on to endure,

Is Inscribed

as a faint tribute of respect and esteem by their
attached friend,

THE AUTHOR.

CONTENTS.

CHAPTER I.

In which the reader becomes acquainted with the family of a Rev. Gentleman.—His daughter, Miss Deborah, advocates extreme views, and her father decides that if his tenantry object to receive what *he* deems to be for their spiritual benefit, he will try the effect of compulsory measures: turn out some of the malcontents, pull down a few cottages, etc. etc.

It is the month of December, in the year 18—; the rain beats pitilessly down in a driving pelting shower; the wind howls mournfully as it sweeps across the hills, and those whom business compels to be absent from home, thread the streets with a rapid step, anxious to gain the shelter of their homes. Yet, wretched as is the night, here and there in the streets of the town of D—— may be occasionally seen small knots of men congregated together, and they ask each other if it be really true, that in the year of Grace, 18—, the Hon. and Rev. Mr. Bishop, the Rector of D——, seriously

B

intends to evict several of his tenantry because they
are guilty of the heinous crime of not allowing him to
tamper with the faith of their children; they whisper,
and they shrug their shoulders; but some of those most
prone to look with an unfavorable eye on the present
state of things, intimate that the Rev. Rector is the
man for any dirty work, whilst a few express their
opinion that fear of scandal, if no better motive, even
supposing his breast to be steeled against every emotion
of charity and pity, will ward off the distressing scene
which it is anticipated will take place very shortly.

But one by one, these little knots disperse; the way-
farers have all returned to their homes, and as the
wind rushes with a melancholy wail over the hills, and
the rain patters against the windows, they draw around
their warm firesides, and thank God that they are not
exposed to the fury of the elements.

But accompany us, gentle reader, to the mansion of
the Rector of D——, the Honorable and Reverend
Mr. Bishop: he is a man rich in worldly wealth, over
and above the good living he possesses. Let us look
within his handsomely furnished apartment, and make
acquaintance with the party there assembled,—for ever
and anon they will figure in the pages of our tale.

There is the Rector, a portly little man indeed, looking like one well contented and on good terms with
himself, and between whom and this world there was
no cause for complaint; secondly, we have the Curate,

Mr. Tomkins, the very antithesis of his superior, a tall spare man, with high cheek bones, small intensely black eyes, peering from beneath a pair of bushy eyebrows, with a lengthened and most sanctimonious visage, looking as though it were a sin to laugh; and with an air of humble deference he yields assent to all his superior's opinions. There, too, are the Reverend Rector's daughters, Miss Deborah and Miss Martha Bishop, the one busily employed in looking over a parcel of tracts, just issued for the benefit of the poor benighted papists by some worthy English folks, who think their money better applied thus, in rescuing the unfortunate Roman Catholic from his idolatry and superstition, than in feeding hungry bodies at home.

Miss Martha is busily employed in looking over the list of papist peasantry who have withdrawn their children from the Rector's School, and comparing it with the account of those who seek the pure light of Gospel truth unblemished by Romish errors, and who have consented to allow their unhappy little papist children to listen to the pure teaching of reformed doctrine rather than give offence to the Rector, and thus incur the danger of eviction, and the certain loss of his favor.

Leaning against the chimney piece, and surveying himself in the glass with a look of undisguised complacency, stood a young man, so like in personal appearance to the Rector, that a stranger would know he was the son of the latter, twisting his moustache with one hand, and with the other taking up the list of disaffected papists, he exclaimed,—

"Mr. Tomkins, I see the Fitzgeralds are amongst those who would not profit by the benefits of pure religious teaching which we have prepared for them. Can you tell me anything concerning the girl, Eva Fitzgerald, who came from England lately on a visit to the old man; I was fairly astonished to meet with an intelligent and really well educated girl in that old farmer's cottage; and i'faith," he continued, "a beautiful girl to boot, with her auburn locks, dark blue eyes, and clear white complexion: see after that girl, Tomkins, papistry must not keep such as her in its toils."

"For shame, brother!" exclaimed Miss Deborah; "is the soul of the girl Eva more precious in the Lord's sight than that of others of these poor deluded people, be they the poorest and most ignorant amongst them? I fear me, John, you have thought too much of Eva's pretty face, and her powers of conversation, than her immortal soul; and after all, Martha," she added, turning to her sister, "really *I* do not see that the girl is so very good-looking; and as to her being able to engage in conversation with her betters, it is only a very great pity that she has been brought up in such a way, just taken out of her own sphere of life instead of being sent out to servitude."

"Jealousy, Martha, and envy," interrupted the

brother, "it is nothing else that makes you speak of Eva in that way."

"Cease this unchristian-like dispute," exclaimed the Rector, in an angry voice; "and look you, John," he added, addressing his son, "were this Eva one of the handsomest and best of women, and as well educated as any lady in Ireland, it shall not save her grandfather and aunt from being turned out with the rest of my rebellious tenantry." Then turning to his Curate— "Mr. Tomkins," he said, "who and what is this girl, my good friend? old Fitzgerald is a very respectable man, and never should I have turned him off my estate but for his obstinacy in refusing with his daughter to send his grandchild to our schools."

"Eva, Rev. Sir, is also a grandchild of Fitzgerald's; his son, a wealthy jeweller, married an English girl, who, as the story goes, was a great beauty, and the daughter they tell me much resembles her: she has two sisters, and while the father lived everything went on well; these girls were being educated as ladies, their father being a wealthy jeweller, and as Eva happened to be the eldest, her education was completed before a reverse of fortune took place; but the father died, and it seems that Eva's mother married again only a few months after his death, whereupon Eva, not liking her young stepfather, very deliberately packs up all that belongs to her, seeks a situation as governess, or teacher in a school or something of the sort, and in

great indignation that her mother should have given
her a Protestant stepfather—or, indeed, a stepfather at
all—my young damsel bids farewell to her mother;
and oh, paragon of dutiful daughters,—oh excellent
papist," ejaculated the Curate, " the young lady—as I
suppose we must term Miss Eva—tells her mother to
send for her when the moment of trial comes, remind-
ing her that she will want her help when her young
Protestant husband, perhaps, will not turn out exactly
as she expects; but the whole of my tale is not told:
I had almost forgotten that there are two young sisters
whom Eva loves very much, but whom she has great
fears will be brought up as Protestants. Oh! a mighty
zealous soul is this Miss Eva, I assure you. I have
tried her several times, but the quiet dignity with which
she endeavours to parry my attacks is really something
amusing. I think it is mainly owing to her influence
with the old couple that Bernard has been taken
from the school, and I really am not sorry to think that
pretty Miss Eva will be punished through her aged
relation."

" Can she help them, think you?" asked the Rector,
"I really did not imagine that any of my Roman
Catholic tenantry were so respectably connected."

" Not she," rejoined Mr. Tomkins; " she saved up
enough out of her salary just to come over here to see
the old man, but depend on it she can't help him to
a night's lodging, she has not a penny beyond what is

sufficient to take her back to England. Wonderfully intimate, too, she is with Father de Vere; a Romanist of the first water is Eva, depend on it, ready to die in defence of her superstitious faith, and maintain her papist doctrines against any and every enlightened clergyman in the three kingdoms."

"Have you seen Joshua Medge lately?" asked Miss Deborah, slowly sipping the wine which had hitherto stood untouched before her; "you will be obliged to have his help, papa, will you not?" she continued, "in order to see that these unhappy people leave their homes quietly. Oh, from my heart I pity them;— what immense trouble poor Martha and I have taken the Lord only knows, to induce these poor benighted creatures to profit by the light of reformed truth, which our zeal has placed in their way, and yet they turn aside, and my heart aches for them, and all I can do is to pray; prayer is all powerful, papa, and may yet win over these obstinate papists, may it not?"

"Yes, my child," said the Rector, "let us be most earnest in prayer, and I have no doubt that though many are refractory, we shall yet win over several of these poor souls to the true fold of Christ. Poor creatures, I grieve over the severe step which, though a minister of the Gospel, I am compelled to take, but it cannot be avoided; leniency would be the greatest fault I could be guilty of; these people must be taught not to dispute my authority, and if they do not know what

is good for themselves, must be taught it, and made to
receive it, too; and there is no safer course to pursue,
I am well persuaded, than severely to punish the rebellious, and as there is a large body of military and
police in the town, I hope all will go off peacefully and
quietly."

"I could have wished that the weather had been less
severe," said Miss Martha; "this inclement season will
awaken a feeling of sympathy even in the breasts of
our Protestant friends, which otherwise would not be
felt."

"For shame, Martha," said the Rector, "do you forget that the Lord sends these heavy rains and piercing
winds? Perhaps He sends them in wrath upon this
deluded people, and it may perchance be that some
rebellious one, may thereby be turned from his evil
ways: yes, it may even be that out of pity for his poor
sinful flesh he may at the eleventh hour seek our cle-
mency; thus it is written that out of evil good shall
proceed, so that which is only done from a base pity
for this poor human nature, shall in the end work
together for good. As for ourselves, for once we rescue
these poor creatures from their soul-destroying superstition, and the teaching of Father de Vere—as they
call him—I have good hope that the light of pure truth
will break in upon them, and they will then for their
soul's welfare become pious Protestants, though they
have only cast aside their papistry for the goods of this

world. So now," continued the Rector, "let us to prayers, my children, particularly remembering these poor deluded persons."

As we have no wish to intrude upon the private devotions of Mr. Bishop and his family, we will bid them farewell for the present, and carry our tale to an English home in the Sister Isle.

CHAPTER II.

A scene from real life.—The English home of Eva's mother.

IT is a December night; snow lays thickly on the
ground; a cutting north-east wind is blowing, adding
double severity to the already sharp frost which has
prevailed for three weeks past; out in the suburbs of
London the cold is even still more sharp than in the
metropolis itself; but we must leave the huge Babylon
behind us, and with the privilege allowed us, peep into
an English home to night.

Standing a little off from the main road in the pretty
village of Croydon, surrounded by a neat and trimly
kept garden, we behold a pretty white cottage; curtains
of crimson damask are drawn over the windows, and
between their folds we can see that there is a large and
cheerful fire in the ample stove, and that the lamp
burns brightly on the table.

But, hark: the snow cracks beneath our feet, and
the easterly wind comes sharply across our face; our

feet and hands are benumbed with cold, and yet, heedless of all, a female ever and anon leaves that warm snug fireside, and so careless of self that she forgets the cold, stands looking out, up that long dark road; she shivers with cold, yet she is heedless, too, for she leans against the garden gate, and sighs very deeply, for he for whom she watches cometh not. Again she returns to the house; but see she is not at rest, for now the crimson curtain is lifted, and that white careworn face peers anxiously forth.

But come with us, gentle reader, let us visit Eva's mother in her solitude, and know for whom she watches.

A fine, nay, a splendid woman is Mrs. Morden still; she has past her prime you see, and yet connoisseurs in female beauty might prefer her charms even before those of Eva. She is forty-five years old, but what matter, that fine form, tall and elegant, bends not in the least; not a grey thread rests in that long dark hair, though they will come anon, for Ellen now begins to feel the touch of grief; see, her head rests on her delicate white hand, her face so beautiful is very pale; the eyes, full of passion, fill with tears, and the well formed mouth, the parted lips, and dilated nostrils, all tell *how* deeply that proud passionate woman can feel. She speaks aloud, and utters the name of Eva. Eva was *once* her favourite daughter; let us hear what she says, for her maids are at rest; the hand of the ormolu timepiece on the mantelshelf points to two o'clock, there is no one to hear her, and she expresses her thoughts aloud.

"Eva, too, to forsake me," she exclaimed, in the bitterness of her grief, "dutiful Eva!" and a sneer sets on that proud lip. "Because I dared to wed so young a man three months after her father's death, and he not a Catholic, *she*, forsooth, must leave me : true, *he* makes me suffer, but what then? A poor excuse for *her;* and those children, Kate and Dora, are not what they should be : Kate too like Eva; Dora, ah, well, too like myself, mayhap, and he—the heartless one—for whom I gave up faith, and fortune, and my child's love and this world's respect, *he* leaves me to squander my fortune, to leave in the end my children and myself penniless; he leaves me for the gaming table; he leaves me—oh, misery—to *myself*."

Ellen Morden presses her cold hand to her burning temples, she goes to the hall door, she looks out into the dark night, she shivers as she re-enters the parlour, replenishes the fire, looks sadly on the untasted viands which for several hours have stood upon the table, and advancing to a sideboard holds up to the light a decanter filled with brandy ; she shudders, replaces the decanter, and turns aside, then again returns, she has overcome her fears, muttering to herself, "I *must* have stimulants, or I shall surely die;" and pours out and swallows a wineglassful of the fiery liquid. Again, another glass, and another, and then she throws herself on the couch still to wait and watch till her lord and master shall return. Ellen is not pale now,—oh, no; a high color burns upon her cheeks, but she is perfectly sober; she is too used to the liquid she has quaffed off so quickly, for it to have affected her head; but she will not watch much longer, of that she is resolved; love has long vanished, fear alone makes the haughty violent Mrs. Morden submissive, and unfortunately that fear forsakes her when she thus seeks to drown her care.

It is now half-past two; she for safety's sake removes the burning mass of coal from the stove, and in a fierce and bitter spirit she takes away all sign of the sumptuous meal which has graced the table, " he shall come home and go to rest cold and comfortless to night," she says, and with a bitter smile on her lips she lights a candle, and is about to retire to rest, when she fancies she hears a step on the crisp snow without; yes, she is not mistaken, it is *his* step—*his* step which she has watched for during many a weary hour that long dreary winter night.

Now, gentle reader, Frederick Morden enters; ah, truly, you will exclaim with us, *that* woman has sown the whirlwind, it is but right that she should reap the storm.

He is young, very young and handsome, too; twenty-seven years old only, that is his age; who can pity his

wife?. Why that man was the shopman of the jeweller
Fitzgerald; he was an apprentice in his service when
Kate Fitzgerald was a baby, and has often had his
master's child on his knee. Ah, Ellen, we cannot pity
thee.

One glance was sufficient; Morden looks around the
room, he bids her relight the fire and bring him food.
With a haughty resentful glance the ill-used woman
points to the timepiece, and asks him if these are fit
hours to keep, bids him seek for his own meal, reproaches him with taking her money to the gaming
table, vents forth in words all the angry bitter thoughts
of that long desolate night.

For the first time he ventures on a speech which
hitherto, brute as he is, he has refrained from uttering,
though the ever busy tempter at his elbow has often
suggested it.

"Fool," he says, "did you think that I so young
wedded myself to your forty-five years from affection?
oh, sweet delusion! No, no, Ellen; I wanted money,
so I endured the wife—now, not a word," he exclaimed,
seeing her about to speak, " but go, and replace what
you have so industriously removed."

Her fiery spirit is up, that inhuman taunt Ellen
nevèr will forgive, body and soul she has been his
slave; but now she will bear no more, she tells him so,
and taking up her candlestick prepares to leave the
room.

But all is not over; Ellen will have far more to endure yet than the loss of worldly goods; this night is the beginning only, the arm is upraised, and ere she is aware of his intention, the clenched fist deals a heavy blow on that beautiful face. Ah, let us close the scene; but reader, we have only taken a page from the sad book of real life, there *was* such a being as the wretched Ellen Morden, and *we* knew her *well*.

Let us leave her in her death-like swoon, it will last until the dawn of the December morning breaks into that home which *should* and *might* have been a home of peace and love, in which the gentle Eva's gladsome smile and cheerful countenance would have shed joy around her, in which her younger children might have grown up with a cloudless unblighted existence, not such an one as she had given them; but no, sober widowhood and a graceful maternity presented no charms to the mind of Ellen, she made her choice, it was now too late to retrace her steps.

CHAPTER III.

In which our friend Eva seeks the Rector, and receives godly
advice which she fails to follow.

On one fine morning in December, when the blue mist
under the influence of the wintry sun rose like a
fleecy cloud over the hills and mountains of Rossmore,
a young and beautiful woman pursued with a hasty
step the somewhat rugged road which lay between the
village in which she resided and the town of D——, in
which dwelt the Rector and his family, whom we have
already had the honor to introduce to our readers; the
morning air was sharp, and a somewhat high wind had
arisen, but the young wayfarer heeded it not, but onward, onward over the ruts of the ill-formed road,
across the hills, then on the level plain, she still pursued her route.

Scarcely above the middle height was this young
maiden; slender and delicately formed; her complexion
was fair, her color heightened by the freshness of the

morning and the rapidity with which she had accomplished her morning walk of six good English miles ; her hair of that fine golden tint which we rarely see save on the head of a child, strayed in natural ringlets over face and neck ; her eyes were of deep blue, shaded by long silken lashes, thus softening down the otherwise hard expression of her features ; for the curved and compressed lips, which though often parted into a smile, together with the slightly aquiline features generally, *could* wear an expression of haughty disdain if our friend Eva's temper got the better of her judgment.

Of a half-and-half kind of race was Eva, half English half Irish. She, the very child of impulse, partook of the vices and virtues of each nation ; she had been born amongst the hills and mountains of D——, of an Irish father and an English mother, the latter of whom we have in the last chapter introduced to our readers ; and whose beauty had won the admiration of the rich Irish gentleman, who was making a tour over the hills and through the valleys of Ellen's native place.

A snug comfortable homestead was the farm in which Ellen's father dwelt, with rich meadows all around, and herds of fine cattle grazing on the pasture, and plenty on the board, and peace and contentment in the heart, and at the time to which we refer, Ellen had but lately left the Convent school. She was not a fine lady then, but she knew how to bake and churn, how to look after

the dairy, and superintend domestic concerns, and keep
the maidens to their work, and see that all went right
as to the domestic management of the farm, for Ellen's
mother had been some time dead.

But when the well-to-do jeweller, whose business
flourished in London, wherein he had made himself a
home, when he offered his hand to Ellen, the case was
soon altered; both father, though he was falling into
years, and farm also, were soon forgotten, and she
loved far better to braid her raven hair, and see the
rich gem sparkle on her well formed arm, than to
place the simple band across the forehead, or behold
her person unadorned.

Thus, then, it happened that Ellen Manton became
the wife of Fitzgerald; who, with the true spirit of a
honest hearted and strong headed Irishman, with whom
success in business had failed to draw out any bad
point in his character, decided on spending the honey-
moon in his native village, in which his father, a small
farmer, had passed many years of his life; here, too,
was Eva born, and here at the request of her grandfather did she spend a few years of her young life, until
removed home for education, which was partly conducted by a superior governess, and then finished in a
Parisian conventual establishment.

But we have made a long digression, so we will
join Eva, who has heard with horror of the threatened
evictions which are to be carried out at D——, and

who now with a palpitating heart approaches the Rev. Mr. Bishop's handsome residence, to plead for a little orphan child, the grandchild like herself of the good old farmer, Bernard Fitzgerald.

Eva was one of those impetuous excitable persons who never can do things quietly and slowly. She was not perfect, gentle reader; oh, no, she was quite the reverse; we, in fact, never pretend to draw such characters, having no accurate notion that they ever existed.

Eva longed to get the visit over; she is about to confront this dreaded Rector and his daughters; she does not fear them, or look up to them as do the poor simple peasantry of D——; she is no ignorant peasant girl, but can very well enter the lists with the proud Rector and his daughters; but Eva is of a proud, excitable temperament, with a disposition peculiarly sensitive to injustice, and therefore it is, that as she raises the knocker at the principal entrance, her heart beats, and her hand trembles, though not so as to cause her to give that tremulous uncertain demand for admittance which would assuredly have sent her away unheard.

Eva was plainly and simply dressed in a dark merino robe, with black mantle and straw bonnet, simply trimmed with a wreath of hawthorn blossoms; but there was a native elegance in her manner that repelled rudeness on the part of the servant who answered her summons, and who stared with somewhat of surprise as

she drew forth a richly ornamented card case, and
expressing a wish to see the Rector, placed a card in
his hand bearing her name; she was immediately
shown into a small parlour whence she could distinguish ejaculations of surprise and murmurs of dis-
approbation; and ever and anon a proud smile sat
upon her lips as her name, now pronounced with deri-
sion, now surprise, struck upon her ear.

At length the door of the room in which she sat was
opened and a servant led the way to the breakfast
room, in which were seated the Rector, his family, and
the Curate.

"It gives me much pleasure to see you, Miss Fitzgerald," said the Rector, rising and offering her a seat;
"we have often vainly wished that it were in our power
to do any good for your aged grandfather, but heaven
has doubtless vouchsafed to your voice and efforts what
it has denied to us; for we can not—will not think that
you seek us save with one great purpose in view both
for him and for yourself."

"I am ignorant as to what you allude, Rev. Sir,"
replied Eva, just sensible to the fact that the Rev.
Mr. Bishop was wilfully misconstruing the purport of
her visit.

"Nay, Miss Fitzgerald," exclaimed the Rector, "I
should opine that it required no very great discernment
to see that with such a mind as yours, highly cultivated—if report speaks truly—that you could not

remain long in your present position; the light of truth, my dear young lady, will break forth, error and darkness must give way in this our nineteenth century, and Rome can only hope to hold subject to her thraldom—which is truly debasing and servile—the souls of those who will never be otherwise than hewers of wood and drawers of water."

" You mistake the cause of my visit much, Rev. Sir. I sought you for one cause alone; and that was to beg of you to do a deed of justice. I cannot—will not believe, Rev. Sir, that it is your intention to turn my aged grandfather off the farm he has so long held, because his daughter refuses to deprive her child of his faith; it is to ask if such be really your intention, to beg of you, in the name of charity and truth, to pause ere you determine on so doing, that I have craved this interview this morning."

" I pity you from my heart, Miss Fitzgerald," said the Curate, " if such be only the object of your visit; I was of the same opinion with our good Rector, and had hoped education had tended to enlighten you as to the errors in which you had been brought up; truly, you are more to be pitied than are those ignorant ones around you, for they possess not the advantages which you have had."

" I come not to argue, sir," replied Eva, rising as she spoke, " if I had presumed on such an errand, I might ask you if the Church, who ranks amongst her

children the noblest and wisest of the sons of men, who
have transmitted to posterity the finest works of genius
and of art, be not in this our own age still loved and
honoured by the noble and the learned as she ever
was; else, sir, how is it that such as these who were
an ornament to English Protestantism have united
themselves to Rome? Is it, Rev. Sir, to make amends
for these defalcations in the Sister Isle, that Irish
Mission Schools are established here, and that Poor
Law Guardians are proselytising through the length
and breadth of both countries the little ones of our
flock, in order that if Rome gains one way she shall at
least lose the other?"

"Even so, Miss Fitzgerald," replied the Rector;
"it seemeth good to us not to leave the souls of these
poor benighted ones to perish without the bread of
life, and none to break it unto them, therefore it is that
we *have* established schools under the auspices of the
Irish Church Mission Society to Roman Catholics; a
godly teacher, too, is Josiah Nosworthy, in whose care
the school is placed, and if your aunt, Mrs. Meara,
relent and send her boy thither, we will consider the
case, and it may be that out of pity to his great age we
may relent and allow your grandfather to remain on
his farm; otherwise, Miss Fitzgerald, you really will
have to take him on your own hands, and it is a hard
world, maybe harder than you think for, if you come to
try it as you will have to try it then. I have no pity

to spare for the rebellious : my Curate and my family, aided by myself, have not opened these schools for so merciful a design to be passed by. I can pity the ignorance of my tenantry, and have provided a remedy for that, which they can by no means avoid; but, for disobedience and open rebellion to superiors I have no mercy; if they will not accept that which is good for them with humble thankfulness, chastisement which they justly deserve will not be wanting."

" I thank you, Rev. Sir, for your unasked for advice," said Eva, gracefully bowing, her proud eye flashing with indignation; "I own the truth my youth and inexperience led me to doubt if all I heard was correct; I had disbelieved that you could ever carry out the threat of eviction which has been levelled against your unfortunate tenantry; but mark me, Rev. Sir," she added, "if this be done, your name will be received with execration far and wide, and the good and pious of your own faith will blush that you, a Christian minister, should bring such scandal on the creed which you and they alike profess."

As Eva spoke thus, she advanced to the door, re-treating amidst the wondering and indignant glances of the assembled company.

With a flushed face and sparkling eye she passed through the spacious hall, out through the door opened for her by a servant in attendance, and took her path across the field which skirted the high road back on her wearisome journey, through ruts and over hills; her vivacity for the time had disappeared, and her woman's heart ached and sorrowed to think of the distress impending over those she loved, and the words burst from her lips:

"My mother, my wretched mother; why, why did you work our ruin and your own by this miserable ill-starred marriage? My poor father's money is recklessly squandered, and I powerless to help this aged man."

A tear filled the eye of Eva as she thus mused, and tired and weary she sat her down beside a hedge, and was soon lost in reflection from which she was interrupted by a voice exclaiming,—

"Whist, Miss Eva! ah, and is it yourself, agra, and your purty face red with a long walk; and its after being tired, you are, so come and have a wee bit to eat and a drop to drink: and tell old Norah all the news, for sure, and I know you have seen the Rector this morning."

"Aye, that I have, Norah;" said Eva, rising from her seat on recognising the voice of an old woman formerly a domestic of her grandfather's, who had been married for some years, but whose heart still clung to her former master, and who never suffered a week to pass by without paying a visit to her former home.

Eva thankfully accepted the good woman's invitation, for she was both faint and weary; and we will leave them together for a time, and return to the Rector and his family.

A mute stare of astonishment sat on the countenances of all, as Eva spoke her few parting words and left the room; and she little deemed that she was closely watched as she retreated across the high road which skirted the grounds belonging to Mr. Bishop's habitation.

" She treads it like a queen," said Miss Martha, with a toss of her head ; " nay, I doubt if our gracious lady Victoria has half the pride and haughtiness that girl possesses. Did you note, Deborah," she continued, " how her cheek glowed, and her eye flashed, when she was arguing with papa? and how she threw back her head with such inconceivable haughtiness, as though she were afraid she would lose an inch of her stature, which is too short to allow her to think she can be called a fine figure ? "

" I noted all," said Mr. Tomkins, " nothing was lost on me : but what room is there for wonder ? See you not she is taught by the minister of Antichrist; the Parish Priest of D—— gives her many an admonition, I warrant me, and they are all persons of the same stamp."

" God be merciful to them," replied the Rector. " And now, girls, I think you had best put on your bonnets, and your brother William and Mr. Tomkins will accompany you to the Mission Schools, and you can inspect things a little, catechise the children a little yourselves, and see how affairs are progressing."

"I will be ready to join the ladies as soon as I have settled a little business for which my presence is necessary, if, indeed, they will favor me by waiting a short time," replied Mr. Tomkins; and the sisters giving a ready assent, he left the room accompanied by the junior Mr. Bishop.

It was, however, full two hours ere the two gentlemen returned, and the whole party then pursued the same route which our friend Eva had taken a few hours before; and the result of their visit we will make known in another chapter.

CHAPTER IV.

In which it appears that Catholic teaching is not so easily dispossessed from the mind as many, like Mr. Tomkins, would desire.—He is startled by a mystery he cannot solve, but comforted in the spirit by finding that the Society have made a *rale* convert of Pat Branigan.

A LOW irregular building was that in which the identical school was kept, which was under the supervision of the Irish Church Mission Society, to which Mr. Bishop had alluded in the morning, and which was situated somewhere about midway between D—— and the Rector's residence.

This school *had* been attended by many wretched children of Catholic parents, who, fearing lest they should lose their all in this world through the bigotry and intolerance of the man who was at once their landlord and the Rector of the parish, had consented to allow them to frequent these schools, established—as

Mr. Tomkins had had the effrontery boldly to avow—
with the purpose of making the children Protestants.

The greater part had, through the zeal and energy
of Father de Vere, the Parish Priest of Rossmore, been
withdrawn, their parents determining to brave the
worst rather than to submit to the tyranny exercised
towards them ; but some few of the poor little *jumpers*
—as they were significantly termed—yet remained.

"Ah, Josiah, my good friend," exclaimed the elder
sister, advancing graciously to meet the Master, " we
have come to see how you are getting on with these
poor children. Mr. Tomkins here will, I have no
doubt, favor us by catechising those whom you think
are best instructed in our Church Catechism."

Four unfortunate boys were then selected by Mr.
Nosworthy as being precocious children, and the poor
ragged little urchins stood up in no small fear and awe
before the inquisitorial Mr. Tomkins, and the ladies,
and young Mr. Bishop.

"How many Sacraments are there?" demanded the
Curate, in a magisterial voice.

"Seven, plaze, sir," answered the boy.

"Wrong ;" replied the Curate, passing the question
down the row. They all replied the same ; when aware
that they had given the answer in the old Catechism
they had been taught three years before, two of them
called out,—

"No : there are only two Sacraments, plaze, sir."

" Right; and what are they ?" he demanded, thinking that he was making some little progress.

" Baptism, Penance, Confirmation, Holy Eucharist,"
repeated the boy in whose mind the well remembered
words still rung.

" Fie upon you," said the Curate. " Mr. Nosworthy,
I hope you do not neglect your charge," he said, as he
drew the teacher half aside; " these children seem to
cling insensibly to their own superstitious creed."

" Yes, as the ivy clings to a venerable ruin," said a
soft voice, which seemed to whisper in his very ear.
He looked around astonished and disconcerted, but no
person was near him, and he resumed his task though
somewhat thoughtful and annoyed.

" It is a great, a fearful sin, my boy, is it not, to give
honor to saints and angels ?"

" It is forbidden to give them supreme or divine
honor," said the boy, faithfully repeating the words he
had heard of old; adding, " for this belongs to God alone."

" Put your Romish Catechism out of your head, sir,
now you have the blessing allowed you of coming here,
and answer me properly: we are not allowed to give
them any kind of honor."

" Yes ;" said the boy, turning red and stammering
from fear and confusion, " we may give them an inferior
honor; this is due to them as the special friends and
servants of God."

" Put this boy aside, Josiah," said Mr. Tomkins, now

really angry; and he muttered to himself, " I'll see whether he answers me intentionally in that way or whether the fiend possesses him with ringing those words so faithfully in his ear."

Mr. Tomkins now turned his attention to the third boy, who seemed more acute than the others, saying to him,—

"You never pray to the Virgin Mary now, my good boy,—you have learned the folly of that sort of thing?"

"Yes, sir; we say the Hail Mary every night, said the boy; it is right to pray to the Blessed Virgin, for she is the Mother of our Saviour."

"Stop, my good lad," said the Curate, whilst the ladies and their brother listened in pious horror, "we have nothing of that sort here; the Blessed Virgin— as you call her—rather the Virgin Mary, was a sinner like every other woman."

"Blasphemer, hold thy peace!" exclaimed a voice again close to Mr. Tomkins, though now so·loud that every one present heard the exclamation.

The Curate was exceedingly wroth; he looked around in hopes of fixing on some boy who was the culprit; but all in vain, the faces of the children wore the same stolid expression, the same surprise was marked on each, and he was about to retire angry and discomfited at not being able to punish severely some unfortunate wight, when Nosworthy exclaimed,—

" Ah, Rev. Sir, a boy is here who I am sure will give

you every satisfaction, he does such credit to our teaching. Stand up, Patrick," he continued, and a bull-headed, red faced boy now stood before the Curate.

Yes, he gave him ample satisfaction ; Pat never forgot himself so as to utter a word of Catholic truth. He was one of those whom the proselytisers love to get hold of; he had attended the schools of the Society from the first; the few first impressions had been effaced, and Pat was a Protestant.

It was now long past noon, and some few minutes before the Curate and his party emerged from the School-house, Eva was cantering along the moors at a pretty brisk pace, on a little black pony which belonged to Dame Cavanagh, and which she not unfrequently used when she happened to stray in that direction.

A merry laugh every now and then rang from the girl, who appeared well pleased with herself and all around her. She had overheard all that had taken place in the School-house, for she had stood in an adjoining thicket, and against a window of the School-house she had leaned the whole time of the examination, her form concealed by the ivy which grew thickly over the window. But Eva recognises a friend in a gentleman in the distance, and that friend is none other than Father de Vere, who exclaims, on her reining in her pony and advancing to meet him,—

"Why, Eva, what wondrous news have you to tell?

You bring comfort, I would fain hope, to our poor people; you look so merry."

" Small comfort, father," replied the girl, " my visit having been as unsuccessful as you predicted; but I will tell you all that has passed."

As Eva spoke she let her pony trot slowly on, and narrated to the Priest the particulars of her visit of the morning.

She was just about to commence her account of the examination of the children, when a gentleman attired in an officer's undress came up, and, bowing to Eva, inquired the time at which it was supposed the evictions would take place.

" Father de Vere," she said, turning to the Priest, " you can better inform this gentleman on every point than I can do; but I must inform you that our good friend has done us much service this morning, and it was the remembrance of the fright he had occasioned Mr. Tomkins, that was causing me no small mirth when I had the pleasure of meeting you."

As she thus spoke, who should cross the opposite side of the road but Josiah Nosworthy; and herself and the Priest heard a voice distinctly calling from the foot of a hill which skirted the road at the point near which Josiah stood,—

" Josiah, both thyself and thy masters are hypocrites, and shall one day share the fate of such."

The Priest stared in amazement: Colonel Monteith, the gentleman to whom we have alluded, looked very serious; while Eva, almost choked from her efforts to conceal her risibility at the mute astonishment of the Mission School teacher, who gazed around him with a sort of stupid surprising, which it was infinitely amusing to observe.

Could it be that party of papists opposite? Oh, how the little man would be revenged on them if he could only swear this was the case; but no, it was impossible, the voice had certainly been close to his side, and the Priest and his party were across the road, and, moreover, some little distance from it, too.

On, then, he went, thoroughly mystified both by the adventure in the School-house and that which had just taken place, and Eva exclaimed,—

"Now for the rest of my story, father: I had just left Dame Cavanagh's cottage, and was lost in thought, letting the pony amble on as she pleased, when I saw the Curate and the Misses Bishop turn into the School-house, and the thought struck me that I would like to see how they taught their children; so, while Jessie nibbled the fresh grass beneath the school windows, I could see and listen to all that passed. But I was not to watch alone, for this gentleman was struck with the same spirit of curiosity, and being endowed with the gift of ventriloquism, he displayed his powers to my, and now to your own infinite amusement, and the evi-

D

dent mortification and annoyance of Messrs. Tomkins and Nosworthy."

Father De Vere was indeed much amused when he heard how creditably the worthy Colonel had displayed his powers as a ventriloquist, for he was well aware that the whole parish would ring, ere twenty-four hours had elapsed, with the account, especially of what had passed in the school.

A short distance only did Eva journey in the company of the Priest and the Colonel who, we ought to have mentioned, was the son of an old friend of her father, and then striking into a path in an opposite direction, soon reached the home of her grandfather.

A venerable looking man was old Fitzgerald; his head silvered with the snows of eighty winters, and with nervous eagerness, leaning on a stick for support, he hobbled forth to hear what news Eva had brought him.

One glance at her face was sufficient; he read the tale she had to tell,—either eviction on the one hand, or to allow the child to be brought up as a bigoted Protestant; or, perhaps, between the two teachings to relapse, as he advanced in life, into a species of godless infidelity, which might very likely be the case.

For a few moments the old man stood perfectly still, musing with his own sad thoughts, then advancing to his daughter he laid his hand upon her shoulder, and said,—

" Mary, my child, dost thou think thou wilt have strength to ' suffer persecution for justice sake ?' for a weary life is now before us ; thou knowest, mavourneen, that the father of thy boy would sooner have seen him stretched dead at his feet than think that son of his should ever be amongst the jumpers. Now tell me thy mind, agra."

" My mind, father," said Mary, " why my mind would be to beg my bread from door to door, with my boy, before I will yield to the tyrant Rector and his Curate."

"God will reward thee, Mary, never fear ; our trial will be a sharp one; we shall feel bitterly leaving our snug and happy home, but happier days may come even here, Mary. And Eva, mavourneen," said the old man, passing his withered hand down her golden locks, "had thy father been alive, neither I nor Mary would have felt this cross so heavily."

" Keep up your spirits, dear grandfather," said Eva, making a rather lame attempt to shake off her own sadness ; " you know I am going to engage as governess in a noble German family, and out of my salary I shall be well able to help you."

Poor Eva, she was young and inexperienced ; she soon felt, however, that it was a far harder task to battle with the world for those she loved than she had ever imagined it would be.

Our heroine had now been a fortnight with her Irish

kinsfolk, and it wanted but two days of the time when she must bid them farewell, for she was about to enter the family of the Baroness von Liebenstein, a rich lady, living at Vienna, who had three daughters, for whom she required the services of an English governess.

It was Sunday—the last Sunday she should hear Mass in that village church for a long time to come; nay, perhaps, Eva would never again see that spot. It is always a painful thing to sever home-ties, more painful still—much more so, if friendless and alone— we have to tear ourselves away. And so it was that all poor Eva's cheerfulness had vanished, and with the traces of tears yet in her eyes, she stood in the little parlour of Father de Vere after the service of the morning was concluded.

"Father de Vere," she exclaimed, when he entered the room, "I have a favor to ask;" and she tried to be very calm, but it was of no use, tears choked her utterance; and then, pausing to command her emotion as she drew forth a rich gold chain, to which was suspended a gold cross set with emeralds, "this," she said, "is the most valuable article I possess: dear papa gave it me on my last birthday, and now I consign it to your care, and desire that when the touch of poverty shall come upon those I love—as it surely soon will—you may kindly apply the proceeds of this bauble to their support. It is most valuable to me as my dead father's gift, but were he living, would he not gladly see me sacrifice it to bring relief and comfort to his own aged parent?"

The good Priest kindly consented to be the medium between herself and Fitzgerald, agreeing with her, that neither he nor her aunt would consent to receive so valuable a present; and Eva then spoke of her home anxieties, her fears for her sisters—both so young—her trouble about her wretched, misguided mother; her doubt as to how the residue of her deceased father's property was being used, her mother having been unfortunately left sole executrix, so great had been the confidence reposed in her by her father. A few months was yet wanting of the time at which Eva, on attaining her twenty-first birthday, could claim her portion as a little fortune for herself.

All these affairs, and many more she freely discussed with the good Priest, wishful to avert till the last moment that dreaded word, "good bye," but it would come after all; and, with tears in her eyes, Eva bade him farewell, and returned to spend a sad evening with her aged relative, for on the following morning she was to proceed at an early hour to Dublin, when after a day or two spent with a friend, she was to proceed on her way.

CHAPTER V.

Showing that women can sometimes imitate the spaniel; and,
by a species of fascination, kiss the hand that strikes them.

SEATED at the window of one of the mansions in Belgravia, with a copy of Ariosto in her hand, is a lady
somewhat passed the prime of life, whilst on a couch
at some little distance reclines an aged and invalid
mother.

The Honorable Amelia Fortescue is that widowed
mother's only child; and they both stared with surprise
as the servant entering, hands a card to the young lady
with the name of Morden engraved thereon.

"How can Ellen make up her mind to come here,
mama?" said Miss Fortescue; "however, I will do my
best to receive her kindly."

Amelia Fortescue was endowed by nature with too
gentle and affectionate a heart voluntarily to give
pain to any one; yet she whose youth, and whose

prime of womanhood had passed in the quiet duties of
the single state, from a principle of duty, almost shrunk
from the wretched Mrs. Morden, who, three months
after her husband's death, formed such an alliance, and
had thus driven Eva, whom Miss Fortescue treated
as a friend—though born in a class beneath her own—
out upon the world.

A glance, however, at Ellen Morden was sufficient;
she looked so pale and miserable, that neither lady
could utter a reproachful word; and Lady Fortescue
and her daughter, who was about Ellen's age, vainly
strove to call to their remembrance the once beautiful
child of Farmer Manton, who had rented one of the
best farms on Viscount Fortescue's estates.

With a nervous step and trembling heart, Ellen
approached the old lady, and stammered forth an apology for intruding on herself and her daughter, adding,

"I am very wretched, and I seek your ladyship for
advice and consolation."

"Who can help you, Ellen, in the fearful straits to
which you have reduced yourself?" said Miss Fortescue.
"There is no help, unless you seek a separation from
the bad man to whom you have allied yourself; we have
already written you to that effect, and can say no more
on this painful subject."

Strange infatuation, the wretched woman made a
gesture expressive of dissent, and then said,—

"I am dying, Miss Fortescue, there can be no doubt of this; look here," she said, and she exposed her arm, now unnaturally thin and wasted; "day by day I find myself growing weaker and weaker, and certain am I that my hours are now numbered; it is about Kate and Dora that I wish to speak; Eva has neglected her duty, and when I am removed who will look to them now she is gone?"

"Eva has only done her duty, Mrs. Morden," rather sharply replied Miss Fortescue, "you make me speak a stern truth: was your second marriage decorous, I would ask? and, secondly, was it seemly? And now, Mrs. Morden, remember the grown up child has ever a hard struggle to receive him or her, whichever it may be, who occupies the place of the departed one; how much more so, then, when the feelings are outraged, as you have outraged Eva's? for scarce was her father three months in the grave, when you marry a man but eight years older than herself. Oh, Ellen, Ellen, you have much to answer for; instead of accusing Eva, you should accuse yourself, who have driven her from her home, and yet," said Amelia, "you will *never* see that it is you who are so grievously in error; is your conscience quite hardened? Why will you be so proud and continue to deny that you have been very wrong?"

"You are very harsh in your judgments of me, Miss Fortescue," said the wretched woman, bursting into tears.

"Then why force me to utter unpleasant truths?" replied Amelia, determined not to yield, "should not your own unhappiness, the loss of your property, the ill treatment that you receive, make you acknowledge that you have deeply erred? why be too proud to own it? And as to the children you have still with you, I should say remove them instantly from so sad a home to some Convent school, and take every measure that still may be in your power to save some portion of your late husband's property for your poor daughters, for you surely were not so silly, at your mature age, to give him power over the *whole*."

"I gave him unlimited power over all that I possessed," said the wretched creature, again weeping violently. "Why, oh, why did Edward place so fatal a power in my hands? did he not know me well enough to be sure it would be used amiss? I am not unlike the rest of my sex; women are not fit to manage such matters."

"I should have some hope of you, Ellen," quietly remarked the old lady, "if I could but see some little sense of humility; but there you are again harping on the same string, blaming every one but your own erring self. Now see us again in a few days, and then let us know that you have sent away these poor children, and are about to separate yourself from the unworthy tyrant you have married."

And Ellen left these two ladies who had been the friends of her early youth, never to return. She yet clung by a species of horrible fascination to the bad man to whom she had united herself. She shrank from the thought of separating herself from her children; she had no peace in her own heart, for she had long since thrown off alike the restraints which religion imposes, and the consolation it bestows, and she seemed to look to these two young girls as a sort of stay, as a something on which she could lean as a support, frail though it was.

Kate Fitzgerald was now sixteen years of age, and strikingly resembled Eva, both in mind and person; to the latter she was tenderly attached, and in her childish fancy she often wove bright images of domestic happiness and peace with Eva, who had bid her dry her tears, for that she would make a little home for herself, and that one day Katie should share it with her. This child was by no means a favourite with her mother, and if we can fancy so odious a passion to find a place in a mother's breast, we may say that jealousy of the affection her two children bore for each other was the cause.

As for Dora, who was one year younger, she was strikingly like her mother. In person she bid fair to be more correctly beautiful than either of her sisters, but her cast of features were like those of Mrs. Morden:

there was the same flashing eye, the same haughty curve of the lip, the same proud consciousness of beauty, outwardly manifested in the very carriage and exterior bearing of both mother and child ; and while Eva and Kate in humility and innocence were all unconscious of the admiration they excited, Dora bid fair, amid her almost regal beauty, rather to inspire disgust than admiration.

CHAPTER VI.

Life's shadows deepen.—The promise and the parting.

LATE on a wet foggy evening in the month of December,
Eva arrived at Croydon, desirous to pay a farewell visit
to her mother before she left England, perhaps for a
long and indefinite period. She had purposely timed
her visit as late as eight in the evening, as full an
hour earlier it was generally the practice of Mr. Morden
to leave home, and adjourn either to the theatre or the
billiard-room, according as his fancy led him.

It may readily be imagined that she shrunk from
meeting this juvenile step-father, to whom her wretched
mother had allied herself; and she had counted on at
least a short hour of quietude and intercourse with
those she loved, before she returned to the friend who
had kindly received her during the very few days which
intervened between her departure from Ireland and
that fixed for her to leave London.

Sadly, however, was Eva disappointed. Her first

summons was not replied to; and when at length the door was opened, the sound of loud voices, with which at times mingled the sweet soft voice of Kate, as though in expostulation, or the louder tones of Dora, in passionate entreaty, told her what sort of an interview she was now to expect.

Unannounced, she hastened through the hall, and opening the door of the parlour whence the voices proceeded, Eva now stood at the entrance, surveying, with mingled feelings of indignation, contempt, and pity, the little group before her.

There, on a couch, reclined her once fondly loved mother; her long black hair had escaped from the net which confined it, and hung in rich luxuriance over her neck and shoulders; her face was deathly in its paleness, for she had fallen into a swoon; but on the white cheek there was a bruise, and the swollen temple also told a tale of cruelty and harshness. Kate supported her mother's head, and the poor girl's tears were falling heavily on that inanimate form, whilst Dora, her face convulsed with passion, poured out a volley of reproaches on the head of the wretched offender, who stood with folded arms, contemplating the fainting form of his wife, with an expression of contempt and hatred on his fine features, and seemingly heedless of the angry words now levelled against him.

But Frederick Morden was a coward at heart, brutal

as he was to his wife; and he felt somewhat uncomfortable, as Eva's calm eye wandered first to her insensible mother, and then to her sisters, and finally fixed upon himself. There was something in that searching glance which he could not bear. He had heeded not Kate's wild exclamation for mercy, as he dealt upon the upraised arm of the girl who strove to interpose between himself and her mother a severe blow, which was intended for the latter; he was deaf to Dora's harsh and angry words, but shrunk within himself as, after a long absence, he encountered—and at such a moment—the girl who, so young a woman, had had the spirit to cast aside all care for the comforts she had enjoyed, and who had avowed her intention to earn her bread as a dependent in the homes of strangers, from the moment of her mother's ill-starred nuptials.

Eva for a short space stood immovable, then advancing to the couch she kissed her mother's pale face, put aside her long hair, surveyed with horror those dark spots *his* hand had inflicted some days since, and advancing towards him, exclaimed with forced calmness —for Eva was the creature of impulse, and it was only by a powerful effort that she could control her temper:—

" This is your work, I presume, Mr. Morden. I have to thank you for preparing me such a welcome home, on this my last evening in England."

" Rather thank your mother, madam," he rejoined,
" whose ungovernable temper drove yourself from home.
Your memory seems short," he added, making for the
door as he spoke, " or you would not forget that on
that account you left your own comfortable home, to
earn your bread amongst strangers."

" Rather say," replied Eva, following, and placing
herself in his path, nothing daunted by the violence of
manner which he now exhibited ; " rather say, sir, I
was driven from my home by my poor mother's unequal
and ill-omened marriage ; that I left her because I
would not stay to witness scenes of brutal violence like
this."

" Forbear, Miss Fitzgerald !" replied Morden. " Not
another word now," he added, placing one hand on the
delicate mouth of the young girl before him, whilst
with the other he grasped her by the shoulder with
almost herculean strength, adding : " Remember now
that this house is mine; that I can turn you from it
this very moment, if I choose ; and as you are, you
say, leaving England, and we may never enjoy the
felicity of meeting each other again, I will say a few
words before we part. Your mother, that woman
yonder," and he pointed to the couch on which the
unfortunate Mrs. Morden, not yet fully conscious,
reclined, " drinks ! Ah ! you shudder; perhaps you
do not believe *me;* well, enquire of those girls, your

sisters, and they will tell you that I speak the truth.
I have shocked you—you, so delicate and refined,
cannot bear this. Well, but listen; I have more to
tell you ere we part. Your pride it was that sent you
from your home, Eva—your detestable pride; you
could not brook seeing your father's shopman in his
place; you could not—would not—own my authority as
master here, as Dora and Kate have done, so your pride
became your punishment. And now, worse news than
all I have to tell you, Eva: look at your mother; see
how haggard and pale she is becoming under her fatal
love of liquor; believe me I speak the truth when I
tell you that, if she died to-night, I believe, Miss
Fitzgerald, you would find you would still have to
devote your talents to the pleasing task of instructing
others, for your mother has been extravagant and reckless. Your father—short-sighted man—nominated his
widow sole executrix, and finely, you will see, she has
fulfilled her trust."

"Monster! desecrate not my dead father's memory
by mentioning his name," exclaimed Eva, as her
tormentor removed his hand from her mouth. But he
stayed to hear no more; he had gratified his malignant
feelings, which Eva had awakened, in an especial
manner.

"Alas! is all this true?" sighed Eva, as she now
stood leaning over her wretched mother, who, restored

to consciousness, stretched out her arms to press in a warm embrace that gentle daughter whom her own mad folly had driven from her home.

Poor Eva! her soul sank within her as she looked on the wan pale face of the mother she still dearly loved—as she gazed on the ravages created by liquor, suffering and care—and she shuddered as she looked on that bruised face, and noted the thinness of the hands and the wasted form.

" Do not reproach me, Eva," whispered Mrs. Morden; " I am severely punished; and my yoke is so heavy, that, were it not for Kate and Dora, I would be thankful if this night I knew that to-morrow's sun would not rise for me. Oh, would that I were dead!" she impatiently exclaimed.

" But you must live, dear mother, for Kate and Dora's sake," exclaimed Eva, " and separate yourself from this bad wicked man, and all may yet be well. Besides, mother dear," she gently added, half afraid to touch on such a topic, yet not shrinking from her duty, " few of us are fit to appear before the holy God thus suddenly; and before I leave you, you will comfort me, I am sure, by telling me that you are not without the Church's pale, as when last we met."

" Oh, Eva love! do not bring spirituals on the *tapis* the few short hours we have to spend together. I cannot satisfy you, darling; I have so much on my

E

mind. I cannot—will not—longer be patient and submissive, when *he* storms at and strikes me, and drags
from me that which is mine alone. I cannot continue
to be good and humble; by and bye, love—a short time
hence. There is time—oh, yes! there is plenty of
time yet; and until then you and Kate will satisfy for
me, you are both *so* pious."

Sick at heart, Eva turned aside to seek for comfort
where it could better be found, viz., in poor Kate, who,
with many tears, gave her a clear insight into all that
had transpired since her absence; and from her and
Dora she then found that the evil temper of Morden
had gained ground by the continued refusals of his
wife to surrender into his hands the whole of the property at her disposal.

Eva adopted much the same plan as Miss Fortescue
and her mother had done, urging on the wretched Mrs.
Morden the absolute necessity there was for her to
separate immediately from her husband, if she wished
to preserve peace for herself, or any portion of their
deceased father's property for her children; and somewhat comforted, though still uncertain as to the strength
of her resolution, she received her mother's promise
that she would not delay, but would leave him that
very week.

Striving then to view this wretched state of things
under their fairest colours, Eva bade her mother and

sisters farewell, and, returning to the home of her friend, busied herself in preparations for her approaching journey, little recking the strange changes which would have befallen *all* of those to whom she was allied by the nearest and dearest of ties, ere she should return to England.

CHAPTER VII.

The evictions.—Might *versus* right.—A saintly minister of the
Gospel.

THE new year has set in; the January of 185- proved
one of the most severe and inclement of seasons; to the
cutting winds, which prevailed throughout great part of
the United Kingdom, were now added heavy and continued rains, which laid the greater part of the rural
districts of this country, as well as those of the Sister
Isle, under water.

In the village of Rossmore matters remained the
same: the Rector and his daughters, the Curate and
the agent, Mr. Forrester, all bestirring themselves, and
making every exertion in their power to induce the
poor peasantry of this and two adjacent villages to
escape eviction by consenting to send their children to
the Church Mission Schools.

The previous spring they had been served with

notice to quit, and during this month—one of the severest and most inclement in the year—it was expected that sixty ejectments at least would take place.

The agent visited Rossmore in hopes at the eleventh hour to induce the refractory papists to submit; the same threat was on the lips of every bailiff, Bible reader, and minister who propagated the Gospel in Rossmore, or for several miles around; and we have now brought our story to the point at which no less than seventy human beings were evicted, and sent to wander through the mountains, in sight of their once happy homes, at the hands of a minister of God, of a Rector of the Church by law established.

We opine that, supposing some one from foreign parts, who knew little of such ways as those practised by Mr. Bishop and his crew, had stopped to rest for the night at some humble way side inn in Rossmore or its neighbourhood, he would have marvelled much why so large a body of the military and police should flock to this poor district where all is at present so quiet; but we would have said to such an one, "Wait, till to-morrow's sun shall have risen, and you will soon see *why* resistance is expected."

The rain pours in torrents; and more than ankle deep do sheriff, and police, and military wade through the flood to the obscure and retired village of Rossmore; the latter take up their position, and the sheriff now approaches the lowly cottage of the first doomed one; the man with his wife and four wretched children are to be turned out; expostulation is unavailing; equally so are the tears of the mother, the cries of the little ones; they are driven forwards; surely, most meek man of God, that woman's shriek is heard by an all pitying heaven. Surely, that wretched man's wild curse might give you cause to fear: but, hark! the clang of the crowbar smites the air; a few moments more, and with a loud crash down come walls, roof and gable; all that was once the home of a poor but honest family.

Away, away again; there is really so much to be done this dreadful morning, that there can be no delay. Another family—five in number—are turned out to brave the fury of the pelting storm. Another and another follow; onwards they go in their work of devastation; and, lo! they come at last to that which is a smiling homestead: formerly there was abundance there, but years have passed on, eighty winters have silvered with their snows the head of Eva's grandsire; his once strong arm is palsied with age, and his worthy son, who would have been the prop of his declining years, has gone long since to his account.

No man ever yet had a word to say to the prejudice of the worthy farmer, in whose character were centered many virtues; but he is not to be spared; and he now approaches, leaning on his stick, his aged form shivering beneath the blast, and tears rolling down his furrowed cheeks. Behind him walks a delicate sickly looking woman, just past, too, her prime; delicate, indeed, to do this world's hard work; this is the aunt of our friend Eva, and she leads by the hand a weeping child, on whose account they are thus harshly driven from their homes, because, in fact, they would not suffer him to grow up an alien to his faith.

At the door of his happy and comfortable home he pauses to take a last look, and tries to utter words of encouragement and consolation to his daughter, but his voice fails him, and sobs choke his utterance; he can only raise his eyes to heaven, and implore its mercy upon himself and those he loves; and mustering up his little strength, accepts the arm of Father de Vere, whose heart aches as he contemplates this man, honorable, upright, aged and infirm, thus exposed to the fury of the elements.

Ah, turn we in horror from the further contemplation of such a scene, sickening and harrowing in its details, which our pen lacks the power, and our will the desire to describe. Let us draw a veil over the scene, which drove on this one day seventy human beings amongst the wilds, and mountains, and hills around their native village; their homes levelled before their faces; themselves and their children driven forth, some of them to die, because they would not betray the faith of their fathers.

Yes, let us draw aside, and blush to think that in

this age of boasted enlightenment, in the year of grace,
18—, such doings can be effected under the shadow of
the law, and, above all, at the bidding of one who pro-
fesses himself a minister of the meek and lowly Jesus.
Yes, let us blush, we repeat, ye men and women of
England and the Sister Isle, to think that our boasted
religious liberty is but a farce, our toleration a delusion, our faith a phantasy, our charity a myth; for
here in the midst of a Bible reading generation, is the
body left to starve and die, whilst Bible Societies are
formed, Church Mission Schools are founded, Scripture
readers are sent on their work, Tract Societies are
established, and lo, all this while love, and charity, and
truth are dead, and as words without a meaning.
Verily, Satan hath set up his kingdom in this world;
and, were it not that we call to mind the long suffering
of God, we might almost marvel how such atrocities
could be perpetrated in the face of a Christian and a
civilized people.

CHAPTER VIII.

Mrs. Morden gives up her children's birthright.—The angel of death approaches.

IT is a mild soft May evening; the sun has scarcely set, and the light fleecy clouds are tipped with many a glorious hue. Down he sinks in his bed of gold, and a soft red light now creeps faintly through a sick chamber which, anon, will be a chamber of death.

All is quiet, now; but yet two hours since there was clamour and confusion, and angry voices there; aye, and sadder still to relate, beside the medicine phial stands the decanter, a fiery draught from which she who dies has but lately tasted.

Beside her mother's couch stands Catherine, and the girl's face is well nigh as pale as is that of the now dying Mrs. Morden. She holds a handkerchief spotted with blood, and the pillow slip, and coverlid, and sheets are marked with the same red tint.

A fearful scene has taken place that day; the wretched, infatuated, and misguided woman, like a spaniel, crouched beneath the hand that struck her; she loved her tyrant, she would not burst asunder the bonds of her misplaced affection; but not she alone shall suffer the penalty and punishment of her own evil doing.

They are alone that May afternoon; none but them-selves are in the house; will not force at last effect Morden's purpose,—"She is very ill and weak, she cannot resist me," prompts the devil of avarice within him. He pauses; he has been very attentive of late, and, musing to himself, thinks that perhaps stratagem will best effect his purpose.

He fetches, then, the liquor which he knows she loves; she needs no urging to induce her to accept the poisonous draught, but raises it willingly to her lips, little deeming that a powder has been infused therein, that so her perceptions may be less acute, that she may be rendered half stupid, and therefore the less able to resist his will.

By soft and gentle words he strove to win her to his purpose, to induce her to give up, to surrender to him-self the last paper which secured to herself and her daughters a small income whereon they might exist, though deprived of many of the comforts they had for-merly enjoyed. Mrs. Morden is half stupid already, between the opium and the liquor she has taken, but

she somewhat sharply refuses; he waits awhile; he
will strive to soothe her still to accede quietly to his
will.

She would sleep, she refuses more feebly; and,
finally, sinks into a heavy slumber.

Stealthily Morden approaches his wife, and feeling in
the pocket of her dress, he abstracts her keys. Then,
like a thief, he crosses the room with quiet step, and
trying several of the keys, he at last selects one which
opens the door of a small cabinet in which she keeps
her private papers.

That sharp click, however, occasioned by his unprac-
tised hand—for he has often vainly tried that lock before, and it has hitherto resisted his efforts—arouses
his wife; she starts, and utters a slight shriek, as she
beholds Morden searching amongst her papers.

He selects that which he desires, and, approaching
her couch, he says :

" Ellen, love, I am so pressed for money, and you
are in want of so many comforts, that I must have
your signature to this paper ; now do not refuse me, I
pray you. I swear by all you hold sacred that your
comforts, and those of the girls shall be duly attended
to ; only sign this paper without delay ; make over to
me this small modicum of your property. Dearest
Ellen, this refusal on your part has alone been a
stumbling block to our happiness, for who but your

husband should in trust hold the property of your
children? Ask yourself if girls young—as are Catherine and Dora—are fit to be left to manage property, in
the event of your death? It is absurd, Ellen, to con-
template so foolish a thing."

The unhappy woman seemed to strive to gather up
her strength for a scene, for she sharply refused; and,
as Morden grasped her by the wrist, intending to force
compliance, she started from the couch, and was about
to raise her voice in angry expostulation, when a stream
of blood, flowing from her lips, choked her utterance,
and she fell back senseless on the couch.

. Hastily the alarmed Morden now called for assistance, and himself placing her on the bed, was so assi-
duous in his cares, so solicitous in her behalf, that the
surgeon fancied this arch hypocrite one of the most
affectionate of husbands.

But the medical attendant has gone, now, and
Morden is again alone with his wife; she is thoroughly
enfeebled and exhausted, and he seizes the opportunity
again. With endearing words, and vows solemnly
uttered, that he will be faithful to the trust she reposes
in him, he urges her to grant his request.

The die was cast. Mrs. Morden's trembling fingers,
guided by those of her husband, traced the words he
required, empowering him to receive her income. She
had yielded to the uncontrollable fascination he exer-

cised over her; and then, letting fall the pen, she sunk
back in a half unconscious state, as her two daughters
entered the room.

The horror of each was, as well may be supposed,
extreme; for the medical attendant had given it as his
opinion that she would not survive many days, and a
return of the effusion had warned all around her that
there was but little time now left for her on earth.

Morden seized the first opportunity to withdraw,
promising a speedy return, and the two girls kept a
mournful watch by their mother's side, vainly breathing
many a wish that Eva were with them.

There is something appalling in the presence of
death, even to those advanced in life, and who possess
stronger nerves than these girls, who were but little
more than children, and Catherine noted, with increasing awe, the change which was gradually overspreading
the fine countenance of her mother.

That she was really dying the poor girl had but little
doubt, and she earnestly implored her to allow her to
summon the Priest of the neighbouring chapel to attend
her, though with little hope that she should succeed;
however, as is not unfrequently the case with Catholics
who have for years lived in the grossest negligence as
far as regards their religious duties, the hold which
the Church has on the minds of her children is
rarely snapped asunder so completely, as that when the
hour of death approaches, there be not some yearning

of the mind, some green spot left in the otherwise sterile soil of the heart, which may yet produce a good thought or some short act of contrition.

Thus it was with Mrs. Morden; and, clasping Catherine's hand within her own, she replied:

"Yes, go quickly; lose no time, for I feel that I am dying."

Catherine would entrust her commission to no one, not even to Dora, but panting and breathless, hastened along the road to the little Presbytery, encountering her step-father on the way. In much surprise at her absence from home, he questioned her as to its cause, and she noticed a smile of contempt pass over his features, as she replied.

A few moments spent with the Priest, who was happily at home, and Catherine again resumed her journey; and ere his arrival, vases had been filled with the freshest flowers, a linen cloth placed on the temporary altar, and wax lights in readiness.

Mrs. Morden had been a weak, nay, a guilty woman; irreligious, haughty and vain, to say the least, and along with the awe which even those who are good and innocent justly feel at such an hour, came remorse at her mis-spent life; remorse deep and bitter, that even that day she had consummated her wrong to her children, by yielding to the will of him to whom she had as it were bound herself body and soul.

For some time the soothing words of the Priest were

vainly addressed to her, but gradually they made an impression ; the days of her youth and innocence, and happy girlhood again returned, and she was received anew into the bosom of the Church, like many of her unhappy children, who put off their conversion till they are at their last gasp.

Ere the departure of the Priest, and after she had received the last rites of religion, she signed to her daughters to approach her, and then declared her wish that they should continue faithful to the practice of their religious duties, charging them to write immediately to Eva, acquainting them with her decease, and also to communicate with their grandfather, for the reader will bear in mind that Mrs. Morden was utterly ignorant of the circumstances that were taking place in Ireland ; and she clung to the hope that the old man might be yet able, in some way, to remedy the evil she had so unsparingly and wickedly wrought.

The Priest had departed, and the shades of evening were thickly gathering around ; the two girls had watched with a sort of nervous apprehension near akin to fear, the rapidly changing countenance of their mother, when they heard the well known knock of Mr. Morden, for which she, too, had long listened.

As something, it may be of regret, shot across the heart of this thoroughly wicked man, as he gazed upon his now dying wife ; and for a moment he reproached himself for his love of the gaming table, and resolved, as he had just made a lucky hit, to frequent it no more. Thus he now felt, and approaching the bedside he took Mrs. Morden's clammy hands within his own, and exclaimed,—

"Ellen, forgive me the suffering I have caused you; I promise to be a father to Kate and Dora; to look to their future well-being, to abjure the wretched vice which has made our home so wretched, only tell me, Ellen, that you are not dying."

But the grey shadow of the angel of death was already passing over the face of his wife; she could not speak, but she pressed his hand, and a grateful smile passed over her wan face, expressing far more than words could utter.

Alas, alas! the gamester's vows are like those of the drunkard, written on the sand, ready to be erased at the first breath of temptation; for few, indeed, are the number of those who are reclaimed from either vice.

For the present moment, however, the gambler's asseverations and promises of amendment answered a good end; they lighteued the hearts of the two lonely girls, who yet almost children, were about to be thrown on his care, and they also relieved of a few of its horrors the mind of his dying wife. He would fain have sent the two sisters away from the death scene, but they so earnestly begged to stay with their mother to the last, that he allowed them to stop; aware, too, that all would soon be over.

Poor children, they had seen their father die, but then all was calm and peaceful. Now, the case was otherwise, and they shrunk back aghast as they witnessed the death agony which was both long and hard.

And the pale May morn had risen and shed her silvery ghostly light over the features of the dying one, who faintly gasped forth the words,—

"Morden, I have trusted thee, break not thy promise, and so shall it be well with thee when the terrors of death shall assail thee; remember thy vow, and that God hath heard thee."

Slowly, and very faintly did these last words of the repentant and unhappy woman fall on the ear of those who listened; a moment more, and the words, "I will remember," uttered by Morden, in a clear firm voice, seemed to stay the spirit in its flight, and then a deep sigh told that all was over.

CHAPTER IX.

In which our friend the ventriloquist occasions no small confusion and much angry feeling, between military and civilians, in the house of our friend the Rector.

It was the evening of the day on which the evictions had taken place, and a merry gathering there was in the house of the Hon. and Rev. Mr. Bishop. Below stairs there was that worthy Mr. Josiah Nosworthy, with his friend, Jonas Stubbs, the Bible reader, and the bailiff, with sundry other persons who had done the dirty work of the morning, and who were all more or less in an inferior grade; whilst the spacious reception rooms above were thrown open for the Honorable Rector's guests, and for whom a sumptuous repast had been prepared.

There, too, were assembled the officers who had commanded the military on that eventful morning, the family of the Rector, the Curate, and several other persons of influence and opulence, whose estates or dwellings were near to those of Mr. Bishop.

The dinner over, and the ladies having withdrawn, the wine circulated more freely; Champagne and Burgundy were poured out with no sparing hand, and the events of the morning furnished theme for conversation.

"I wonder how many of those rascally papists now repent of their choice," said one of the gentlemen; "they have preferred to suffer rather than embrace the pure light of Gospel truth. It is to be hoped that the sight of what they now go through will prove a warning to others."

"Truly, ours was a most gallant charge," said a voice, in a satirical tone, apparently proceeding from an officer named O'Hagan, who, as one of the most zealous ministers of his congregation, was much esteemed by the Rector beside whom he was seated, adding, "I really felt somewhat ashamed of the post we were compelled to fill."

"What did you say, captain?" exclaimed the Rector, in a tone of surprise, and his exclamation was re-echoed by twenty voices, the owners of which looked extremely wrathful, and many of whom held their glasses half raised to their lips in wondering astonishment as to whether O'Hagan was really in the possession of his senses or not.

"Gentlemen," said the unconscious O'Hagan, rising,

and looking extremely red and angry, "I really know
not what you all mean; I have never spoken a word;
why do you all look so angry at me?" added the dapper
little man, waxing more wrathful as he proceeded.

"Well, you really cut a very wretched appearance,"
said a Mr. Hayes, one of the very pillars of the Church
in those parts; "don't be ashamed, captain, of owning
your principles."

"*My* principles, sir," vociferated the little man, in a
stentorian voice; "*my* principles are, that we are bound
to exterminate Popery, at all risks, and at any rate;"
and, forgetting for the moment that he held a glass of
wine, he dashed it into a thousand atoms, by the violence with which he thumped his clenched fist on the
table. "And now, sir," he added, advancing to the
terrified Mr. Hayes, "understand that I shall not
allow you to insult me again, by hinting that I am
ashamed of my principles; and ——"

"Hush—hush, gentlemen," said the Curate, "pray
don't forget yourselves; it must be owned, you know,
that your charge this morning was not at all a gallant
one, as Captain O'Hagan satirically intimated, though
now ashamed of his own words."

The hubbub that prevailed, as the Curate thus spoke,
was truly dreadful. The Rector's voice could not make
itself heard; the military, who had been called out to
keep the peace, lest any of the poor creatures should
rebel under the cruelty exercised towards them, were

now excited to the utmost. They considered themselves most grossly insulted; and some few of the
party scrupled not to aver that the gentlemen had drunk
too deeply,—the Curate amongst the number.

In vain did Mr. Tomkins protest that he had not
uttered the words attributed to him; in vain did he
grow white, as the neckcloth he wore, with suppressed
rage; the voice was that of Mr. Tomkins which had
uttered those offensive words, and none other: and the
dispute was in no wise ended by several of the party
exclaiming,—

"It is no use to deny the words you used, sir, any
more than for Captain O'Hagan, or our good friend
Mr. Hayes; the fact is, you have all drunk too freely."

Then, amid the general confusion, the Rector arose,
and raising his hand to petition for silence, he exclaimed, only half heard amidst the general hubbub:—

"Gentlemen, it is unfortunately clear to me that
many of you are all the worse for liquor; this scene is
in the last degree discreditable; let us break up our
party, and expect a reunion on some future occasion,
in a manner more seemly in the house of a Christian
minister."

"Ha—ah—ah!" loudly laughed Captain O'Hagan,
who had again resumed his place beside the Rector.
"No need to be squeamish, Rector, after the scene of
this morning."

"Do you mean to insult me, sir?" replied Mr. Bishop, himself now roused; but quickly mastering the anger which he felt, he again intimated to the assembled party his wish that they should adjourn their unseemly dispute to some more fitting quarter.

It was some time, however, before the din was quelled; and even when the war of words was over, the war of passion still raged fiercely in the breasts of those who had met with such very different feelings that evening. One thing was certain, and that was that the civilians and the officers were fairly pitted against each other, and when the staunch Low Churchman, Captain O'Hagan, was on his way home, with a few of his brother officers that night, he was even led—much to their astonishment—to express his belief that perhaps *they* were not so right, nor the papists so very wrong as he had heretofore supposed.

"You speak rightly, Captain O'Hagan," remarked a brother officer—our old friend Colonel Monteith—whose arm O'Hagan held; "do you not think, now, that some of our Protestant friends, if the tables were turned, would have given us ample room for the exercise of our duty, instead of bearing it as patiently as did those poor fellows this morning?"

"Yes, I think they would," unhesitatingly replied O'Hagan, to the infinite amusement of those who heard him, for he was as firm as one of the puritans of old, and had often entered the lists with the gallant colonel, when disputing concerning the soul-destroying system of Popery, as he generally called it.

Dear reader, how little did the captain, or the Rector and his friends know that it was to the mischievous powers of Colonel Monteith that they owed the disturbance of the evening.

Verily, he had not exerted his powers of ventriloquism uselessly.

CHAPTER X.

Sudden reverses.—The execution.—A peep into a Poorhouse.

SIX months have passed away; and, in that short space of time, strange events have taken place.

Eva has returned to England, having spent the greater part of the time she had been absent in St. Petersburgh, in which city business had demanded the attendance of the Baron von Liebenstien, in whose family our heroine held the situation of English governess.

The grief of Eva may well be imagined when she heard from Kate of the death of her mother; but the girl's letter spoke so hopefully of the future, and in such enthusiastic terms of the kindness of her stepfather, that she strove to dispel the unpleasant thoughts which crowded on her mind relative to the disposition of her deceased mother's little property, her portion of which she could now shortly claim, having just attained her majority.

Arrived in St. Petersburgh, the correspondence between herself and her sisters necessarily became far less frequent, and the distance of time in receiving the letters of each much longer than heretofore; and when his business was settled, the baron removed somewhat hastily to Vienna. Eva never—perhaps fortunately for her own peace of mind—received a letter which had been written by Catherine, in a moment when the girl's feelings were wound up almost to madness.

Mrs. Morden had been dead about two months, and the kindness of their stepfather had in no degree diminished; but Kate and Dora both noted that on a sudden his old habits had returned, and that, if possible, his hours were later than even in their mother's lifetime. Then he became gloomy and abstracted, and shut himself alone for hours in his room; sometimes not seeing the two sisters for whole days together.

At last came the hour of trial: and a sharp and bitter one it was even to the gentle Catherine, more especially so, then, to the proud, passionate Dora. Nearly a week had elapsed; Morden had one day left home as usual, and had never returned; several times persons had called at the house, insisting on seeing him, and answering the sisters with coarse familiarity, when they declared he was absent; then the house was searched in the presence of the terrified girls, who also observed that it was closely watched.

At last the sad finale came; miserable and dejected,

expecting, and doomed not to receive a comforting letter from Eva, the sisters sat alone, each endeavouring to cheer the other, when they heard a loud knock at the door, and the next moment they were informed, by two coarse featured men who entered, that they were empowered—through the intentional absence of Mr. Morden—to seize upon whatever the house contained.

In speechless horror the wretched girls clung to each other; what should they do? To whom could they fly? Alas! the misconduct of their erring mother had alienated from herself and from them every one whom they could call a friend. They thought of rushing to the Priest, who could at least have given them his advice, but they knew that he had gone away from home for a time; and, in utter desolation of spirit, they wept away many a weary hour.

"Had they no relations?" they were asked, "surely, if Mr. Morden was so cruel as to abandon them, they had other relations to whom they could apply."

"Alas! no;" they replied, "they had a grandfather in Ireland, a sister in St. Petersburgh: but, surely," urged Kate, "we can stay here till we can hear from them. This property was all mama's, and was to be ours; surely, you have no right to take it all for my stepfather's debts."

"It must all go, my dear young lady," said one of the men, touched by the simplicity and distress of these

wretched girls; " but don't take on so, for I'll see that
you be safely lodged till you can hear from your friends;
sure enough, the very name will sound hard in the
ears of them as has been brought up so well, but what
can't be cured must be endured; and, as I know the
master of —— workhouse, I'd advise you both, as a
friend, to cheer up, and I'll warrant I get you comfort-
ably lodged."

" The workhouse!" ejaculated both sisters, in the
deepest dismay. "Gracious heavens! we can never
enter such a place as that."

" Well, but my pretty dears," replied the man, with
an impudent familiarity, which wounded the delicate
Catherine, as it exasperated the proud Dora, "you see
you have no choice; to the workhouse you must go, or
turn out in the streets; and, instead of giving yourselves
airs, you ought to be much obliged to me for offering to
introduce you to my friend. Why, bless my soul," he
added, "don't go for to give yourselves such airs;
ladies, quite as good as you, have died in the poorhouse
before now."

" I'll not go to the horrid workhouse—I never will!"
exclaimed Dora, with passionate vehemence. Oh,
Eva—Eva!" she exclaimed, "why are you not here?"

Then, the remembrance of her mother's error flashing across the girl's mind, she added, "My poor,
wretched mother, what a fate did your second marriage
doom us to undergo."

And those two girls—almost children as they were—
remained in the house when only its bare walls were
left to them; and then, when they had walked till they
were weary one fair spring evening, and knew not
where to rest their heads, and as the shades of night
began to deepen around them, then the two girls sought
with aching hearts, the man who had promised them
the refuge of the pauper's home; and, one hour before
midnight, the doors of the workhouse of —— parish,
in one of the districts east of London, opened to receive
Catherine and Dora Fitzgerald.

The feelings of the proud, impetuous Dora may be
better conceived than described, as with haughty mien
and flushed face the young girl followed the matron,
and the gentle but unhappy Catherine, to the miserable
chamber allotted for their use.

"You will use this room," said the matron, "for
our friend tells my husband that you have been
gentlefolks like, and won't become chargeable to the
parish; so we don't intend to put you with the paupers,
the short time you stop here, and I will talk again
with you in the morning, and see what can be done for
you. In a few minutes I will let you have some re-
freshment, and I shall send for you to-morrow."

Little appetite had the two girls for the supper of
stale bread and butter which was in a few minutes
brought to them, and then, throwing themselves on the
hard bed, they sobbed themselves to sleep.

On the following morning the matron, true to her word, sent a woman to bring Dora and Kate to her apartment; the *debris* of Mrs. Jennings' breakfast and that of her husband had not yet been removed; and Dora's eyes involuntarily fell first on the adjuncts of an excellent meal—such as she had not for some time tasted—and then on the portly form and fat round face of the master, who, ensconced in an easy chair, took off his spectacles, then wiped, replaced them, and fixed a scrutinizing and intent gaze on the countenances of the two maidens, who had been so strangely placed in his care for long or short time, as the case might be, by his friend.

"You will give me the addresses of your friends," he said, to the shrinking girls, "and while we wait to hear from them, I will lay your case before the Board of Guardians, and see in what way I am to act about you. St. Petersburgh," he muttered, musingly, as he repeated the name of that city after Dora: "ah, yes—bless me—somewhere in Russia—hem—a long way off.—Ireland, too; but do you know no one in London who will take you in, or do something for you?"

"My mother knew one rich lady," replied Catherine, with a sigh; "she lived in Belgrave Square, I believe, but I have written to her and received no answer."

"Well, what can't be cured must be endured," replied the master. "My wife will find you work while you stay here, and I will speak to one of the guardians

about you to-day; for you see as how I have no authority to
take young women in, unless they be classed as paupers,
and I don't think your hands look as if they ever done
a day's work yet; and, if so be your friends don't turn
up, and you fell on the parish, work would have to be
found which such as the likes of you will scarcely
fancy."

Kate, by a strong effort, mastered the inclination she
had to burst into tears, whilst Dora exclaimed,—

"I must beg you not to couple our name with such
an idea as that which has entered your mind; we are
not destitute of friends, painful as is our present position, nor need educated young ladies throw themselves
on the parish."

"Though glad, it may be, to have the relief it will
extend for the present moment," replied the man, with
something approaching to a sneer, curling his lip as he
spoke. "However," he added, "proud as you be, young
woman, I really pity your situation, and will, as I have
promised, speak to one of the guardians to-day."

"To be pitied by such a man as that;—to be pitied
by a thing so intensely low and vulgar," were the first
words Dora uttered, as she flung herself into a chair,
on re-entering the small room destined for her use.
"Oh, Eva—Eva! why—why is it you do not write to
us?" she added, "and grandpapa—he, too, is quiet:
what does this horrible silence mean?"

It was some time before the more gentle Catherine

could quiet her unhappy sister; a fresh outbreak of temper—not without some reason—breaking out on the matron refusing to let her go out, and telling her that whilst an inmate of the workhouse, she must consent to submit to the regulations of the place in question.

The following day, too, brought a fresh annoyance to Catherine, which, however, was less severely felt by her sister, save in so far as it galled her haughty nature to meet with any restraint, or encounter any impertinence.

It was Sunday morning; and an exclamation of pious horror broke from the matron's lips, when Catherine ventured to beg that herself and her sister might be allowed to go to Mass.

"It cannot be," she replied; "there are some few Romanist paupers in the house who have permission to attend their own place of worship, but at the hour of nine in the morning; it is now nearly eleven, and I cannot break through any of our rules: you can attend the service of our Church, if you please.

Catherine felt the denial keenly, and drew aside in tears; whilst Dora indignantly refused to accompany the matron, and sadly enough wore away the first Sunday morning in the poorhouse of the Parish of S——.

CHAPTER XI.

Dora's first step to Proselytism.—This Chapter also sheweth
some of the difficulties which attend the Priest in his duties
to the Catholic poor in the Workhouses; and that the
reader may apprehend fully the nature of the obstacles
thrown in his way, we beg to add that we have copied it
verbatim from the journal of a Reverend friend into the
pages of our MS., the chief incidents of which are, we also
assure them, literally true.

THE sisters had resided more than a month in the
Union workhouse, and as yet had heard no tidings of
Eva, of their stepfather, or of Mr. Fitzgerald ; and even
the patient, trusting Catherine felt her heart grow
heavy and sad.

The young girl, too, was beginning to suffer from the
proselytising propensities of Mr. and Mrs. Jennings,
who, deeming that they were performing a most holy
work in endeavouring to weaken the faith of the two
girls, so strangely thrown on their hands, never left
them long at peace.

Poor Kate, too, felt very grievously the little resistance Dora offered; she had, in fact, very quickly become a great favourite with the matron, despite the passionate hauteur with which she had behaved on her first entrance into this detested house.

The weak, vain mind of the young girl was, however, soon touched by the flattering words and conciliatory demeanour of Mrs. Jennings, who praised her beauty, listened with such a gratified air as Dora's fingers swept the keys of the instrument belonging to her daughter; and ended by oftentimes lamenting that she had been brought up a Romanist, and thus rendered unfit to discharge the duties of governess to the children of an amiable lady, to whom she would otherwise have introduced her. In due course of time, however, notwithstanding these lamentations, Dora *was* introduced to this lady, who happened to be the wife of one of the great men of the parish, and also one of the guardians; who, dressing the bait with honied words, and flattering the vanity which she saw reigned paramount in Poor Dora's mind, finished the work Mrs. Jennings had so zealously began.

" We will engage you as nursery governess for our children, at a salary of £20 a year, for a commencement," said Mrs. Bennett; " but our house shall be in truth your home, and you will be treated by me as though you were my eldest daughter; if you choose to enter my family on my own conditions, and these are,

G

that you consent to accompany us to Church on Sunday, and join us at family prayer. Now, hear me out," she added, seeing that Dora was about to speak, and noting, too, the flush which mantled her cheek: "foolish girl, surely we cannot admit as one of ourselves, a young person who really clings to the superstitions of Popery. However, if you like to come, rest assured we will not force your conscience; you may choose to accompany me at a later period. I trust in the Lord, Dora, that you will have light and grace to recognise the truth. Say, now, will you come under these conditions?"

"I will, madam," said Dora, with a faltering voice, for she caught Catherine's eye fixed on her face, and she heard her murmur the words—

"Oh, Dora, what will Eva think of this?"

But Dora thought only of present miseries,—of the horribly humiliating position she at present occupied; she was fascinated by the engaging, affable manners of Mrs. Bennett, and she affected not to hear poor Catherine's remark; but turning, ere she left the room, she embraced her sister, exclaiming,—

"Dear Kate, I hope you will soon be as fortunate as I am, for I am certain I shall be very happy with this warm-hearted lady; or rather, Kitty, I hope Eva will soon answer our letter. Nay, don't look so sorrowful," she added, "I am not going to become a little Protestant all in a hurry, though you know I was never as pious as Eva or you; but I can take care of myself, I assure you."

Thus speaking, the vain, thoughtless girl hastened from the room; and, arraying herself in the best of the few simple articles she still possessed, rejoined Mrs. Bennett, who really gazed on her with unfeigned admiration; for Dora Fitzgerald's beauty was of that brilliant nature that none could pass it by unnoticed. The girl might have been born to be an empress, was the inward thought of the rich citizen's lady. Not one jot of a stature, unusually tall for her age, did Dora lose; whilst her figure was at the same time faultless in its proportions; her features were of the Grecian cast; her complexion delicately fair, whilst her hair was the hue of the raven in its blackness, whilst those long silken lashes, overhanging a pair of large black eyes, softened their expression; and Dora was, in fact, unfortunately for herself, a beauty in the real sense of the word.

Luxury reigned supreme in the home of the wealthy Mr. Bennett, who boasted of a town house in Belgravia, a country seat in Shropshire, and of being the head of a certain wealthy firm in the City; and the internal management of the rich citizen's household was conducted in a style of luxurious extravagance, such as we in vain look for in the establishments of those far above the Bennetts in the social scale.

Naturally a warm-hearted, though a thoroughly

worldly woman, in the strictest sense of the word, Mrs. Bennett's heart had been softened as the matron, once her nurse, related the story of the Fitzgerald's ; yet, it was with a start of manifest surprise, that she received the girl whose carriage, beauty, and general bearing would have become a station far beyond that which she was by birth destined to fill ; and as she was a staunch Church woman, and not well educated enough to have divested her mind, in more mature years, of the prejudices of early teaching, she thought within herself that she should be performing a doubly meritorious act if she took Dora into her care, counting with the pleasure of a naturally warm heart on the delight she should experience in befriending a protegée likely to be so attractive as Dora, and, at the same time, rescuing the girl from the trammels of Popery.

As to Dora, we must own the truth, she was not of an affectionate disposition ; but, as we have already said, vain and frivolous in the extreme, and she felt too much delighted by the novelty of her position, and the luxury of her new home, coupled with the blandishments of her protectress, and the winning ways of her little charge, the darker points in whose disposition had not yet peeped out to have any fear for the future.

True, she *did* weep when she bade Catherine farewell, to think that she must yet stay some time longer in so odious a place ; but those tears were but few, and quickly dried away.

As to Catherine, a deep and settled sadness took possession of the girl's mind after the departure of Dora; her health, never strong, had become visibly impaired during the few past weeks, and a few days later she was confined to her bed, and was suffering under an access of nervous fever.

Poor Catherine's lot was, indeed, a hard one; indebted in this home of the destitute, for the few and slender comforts she enjoyed, only to the kindly feelings of the matron; there on sufferance, liable at any hour to be in very truth placed amongst the pauper inmates; forsaken, by Dora, her own dearly loved Eva so strangely silent, what room for wonder, that the poor head throbbed with pain, or that the flush of hectic fever burned on the cheek. One wish, too, was so dear at her heart; this she knew not how to gratify, for the matron's bigotry, and the proselytising influences around her, often checked her when she was about to express her wish to see a Priest; yet, one morning when so ill that it seemed to her that nature was slowly fading away, and that she might die in that pauper home, she summoned up her courage, and begged the nurse to ask for the attendance of a Monk attached to a neighbouring Mission, to whom the spiritual care of the paupers of S—— workhouse was confided (at least as far as the master and his wife chose to allow him to interest himself in their behalf).

But Catherine was not in the pauper ward, she had

not even the poor opportunity afforded her which the
inmates of the house enjoyed, and it was to a providential chance alone that she at last gained her point.

It was now the middle of june; the weather was
intensely hot, and there was much sickness in the
workhouse wards. Weary with much walking amongst
the courts and alleys with which the localities around
the north-east of London abound; sorrow stricken at
the thought of the misery he had that morning witnessed, a Catholic Priest presented himself at the
office of the master, requesting to see a woman whom
he supposed to be dying. Mr. Jennings' round red
face grew redder than usual on perceiving that the
intruder wore that sign of the ring dove, the Roman
collar, and he insolently exclaimed,—

"Your visits are very frequent: who sent for *you*?—
Is any one sick?"

The Priest mildly replied, "That he had been that
morning asked to see a person who was in danger of
death in the infirmary."

"I know nothing of friends, messages, or letters to
you. Did *I* send for you?" exclaimed the master, in
angry tones.

"That is not the question," firmly replied the Priest,
"the woman, I understand, to be dying, and I must
see her."

But learn, oh Catholic rate-payers, that the poor Priest,
ere he hastens to aid the dying one, must stay to hear

the resolutions of a Board of Guardians read to him ; and this Board resolved, that Mr. Jennings was to inform the Priest *when* his ministrations were required ; and that he was to see that he departed immediately after he had fulfilled them.

"But," added Mr. Jennings, his countenance now wearing one of his blandest smiles, "I have no objection to your seeing this poor creature. I respect you as much as any other minister of religion, but I am acting in my official capacity ; in future, you must only come when *I* send for you."

Vain was all expostulation on the part of Father Lawrence ; in vain did he represent to him that the ministrations of a Catholic Priest were *perpetually* required by his people ; he again received the answer, that in this individual case he should not be interfered with, but that hereafter the resolution of the Board would be carried out.

In the ward of the hospital the good father met the surgeon, who telling him that there was no immediate danger in the case in question, he deferred his visit a few days later ; and, in the interim, he received a visit from a poor Irish woman who, in the room occupied by Catherine at the time when the latter preferred her request to Mrs. Jennings, which was met by an evasive answer, determined on communicating with the Catholic Chaplain who attended the workhouse. To the

workhouse, therefore, on the following Wednesday, the
Priest turned his steps, and meeting the master in the
entrance hall, was at once accosted with—

"Well, sir! who sent for you? Did *I* send for
you?"

"No," answered Father Lawrence, "but as there are
inmates here under my care, I have called to see
them."

"And, pray, did I not tell you," replied our friend
Jennings, "that when you were wanted you would be
sent for?"

"Yes," replied the Priest, "but I happen to be
already in attendance on the people whom I wish to
see to-day: and I have also heard of another case, in
which—a young lady I must call her—though she be
an inmate of this poorhouse, is seriously ill, and has
requested the aid of a Catholic Priest."

For a moment Mr. Jennings hesitated, evidently
well inclined to debar Father Lawrence from seeing
Catherine; but he was aware that that very morning
the doctor had declared that it was extremely doubtful
whether she would recover; and the fear of what might
transpire, in the event of the poor girl's death, tri-
umphed over his bigotry, and won the day for Father
Lawrence.

The fever was at its height when Father Lawrence
entered, the poor girl scarcely conscious, the spirit

hovering, as it were, on the confines of another world ; yet, when he bent down his head, and whispered the words—

" You are a Catholic, and have wished the attendance of a Priest of your Church," the failing senses seemed to gather renewed consciousness, and, pressing his hand, she murmured the words,—

" I am so glad to see you,—I think I am dying,—they would not send for you before." Then, relapsing into a species of delirium, she called wildly on Eva, reproached Dora with cruelty, and sank into a state of insensibility.

Much distressed, the good father, having ascertained that there was no immediate danger, wended his way home, resolving, despite the anger and frowns of Mr. Jennings, to obtain admittance to the workhouse early on the following day.

On returning to his home, too, Father Lawrence carefully re-perused a letter he had received some time previous from the Board, in which he found it clear that applications of Catholics for the ministrations of religion, were *not* to come wholly through the master; and he therefore determined on visiting Catherine the following morning, and recalling to the mind of Mr. Jennings the explanation the Board had given to the resolution.

The worthy Mr. Jennings was in his office, his wife standing beside him, when the Priest entered.

" I think you misunderstood," said Father Lawrence, " the resolution you read to me the other day. A letter I have previously received from the Board bears quite a different explanation, and there is not a word said therein about *every* application being made through you; but quite the contrary, a just and liberal explanation of this letter, grants *everything* I have asked for, allowing me to speak to a sick person—if asked to do so—whilst visiting another in the same ward; all the Board requires evidently being that the master of the house should be satisfied that there existed a desire on the part of the Catholic inmates to see *me*."

As Father Lawrence thus spoke, Mrs. Jennings, who could no longer keep silence; and who, in fact, had all along been bursting with a desire to speak, exclaimed,—

" But the nurse applies when the doctor is wanted, can she not apply when *you* are required ?"

" Well, I rather think the cases are not quite parallel," replied Father Lawrence, " I fancy there is somewhat of a difference between the occasional need of medical aid, and the *constant* necessity for spiritual ministration."

" *Indeed*," exclaimed Mr. Jennings; " *then*, you will allow me to judge, for the future, *when* I consider your ministrations requisite."

The pale face of the good Monk for a moment flushed at this insolent reply, to which he made answer, that he certainly could not admit of the competency of the master to judge in such a question.

" Well," replied Jennings, momentarily waxing more and more wrathful, " I think I ought to have *some* voice in the matter, but I would advise you to appeal to the Board."

" I have so done," replied the Priest, " and have read to you its decision, showing you that it was received by me at a later date, and in fact is an explanation of the resolution 'you have referred to."

" But you come so often," spitefully exclaimed Jennings; " this is the third time you have been here this week, and no other minister of religion, except the Chaplain, ventures to set his foot within this house without my having sent for him."

" The nature of the case is widely different," mildly remonstrated the Priest, " the ministrations of religion required by the Catholic, are different from those of other persuasions."

" I am not going to enter into *your* religious questions," replied Jennings, " I am concerned with the good order of the house; you have been here three times this week."

" You are mistaken," replied the Priest, with wondrous calmness; " I called yesterday to see *you*, and a young girl whom I was told was dying; and have called again to-day for the same purpose. I surely, with many other duties, *should* be allowed to come at any reasonable time, but ——"

"Is *this* a reasonable time, think you, when the inmates are at dinner," broke in Mrs. Jennings.

"I did not call to see *them*, but one who may be now at the point of death, and also the master," interposed Father Lawrence.

The naturally red face of Mr. Jennings grew almost purple with anger, and lashing himself into a rage, he exclaimed,—

"I should advise you, Sir, to butter your words a little when you want them to be swallowed down by a woman." Then clenching his fist, he added, pointing to his better half, "I tell you that's my wife, Sir, that's my wife; and whatever dignity, whatever gentility you may claim for yourself, you shall not insult my wife."

The good Monk could, for a moment, scarce imagine that anything he had said could have excited, to such a degree, the violent anger of Mr. Jennings, and he replied,—

"This is all very well, if any one *did* insult your wife, but ——"

"I'll tell you, Sir," interrupted the little fat man, "if you were the very fiend," he added, striking his fist on the desk, "though you call yourself a minister of the Gospel, you shall not insult my wife; if you were Prince Albert himself, you should not insult her."

"What mean you," said the Priest, "by addressing me thus? *I* had no thought of insulting your wife; what have I said to lead you to mistake me in such a manner?"

"What did you say?" replied the master, "did you not say you came to speak with *me?* And she has as much right to be heard and have a voice as any other person; she is the matron of this house, Sir; she is the matron of the house and my wife."

The Priest was, as he well might be, overcome with astonishment by the scene into which he had so unwittingly engaged, and anxious to close the interview, exclaimed,—

"You are utterly mistaken; I called to speak with a dying person, and with you; and you are not at dinner, are you?"

"No, Sir," replied the excited Mr. Jennings, "I am *not* at dinner; and you should not sit with me at my table, I can tell you. I *can* manage with your Vicar; I *can* talk with him (thus he designated the Confrere of Father Lawrence), but you're too subtle—I tell you that you're too subtle for me."

Father Lawrence shrugged his shoulders, and most probably thinking that anything he could say would only tend still more to excite the ire of the excellent master, he wended his way to the room in which poor Catherine lay.

The fever was somewhat subdued, and now conscious, though in a very weak and languishing state, poor Kate received with much pleasure the good father, who approaching her bedside now listened to the story she told him, broken as her narration was by the excessive weakness of her frame, which prevented her from saying more than a few words at a time, after which Father Lawrence received her confession, and then promising to bring her the Holy Communion in form of Viaticum the following day, he bade her farewell, at the same time adding, "keep your mind perfectly calm and still, I will look to your interests, and should you not see me for several days after my visit to-morrow, do not be alarmed, for unfortunately my egress here is anything but pleasant to the master of the house; only remember," continued the good priest, "I shall bear you and your interests in mind," and then giving her his blessing, Father Lawrence departed.

CHAPTER XII

Eva's return.—The evening of a weary life draws to its close.
—Delusions of Fitzgerald; his visits to the old homestead.

THE almost stifling heat of a July afternoon had been
succeeded by one of those heavy storms which so beautifully cool the fervid atmosphere at this season of the
year, a refreshing breeze had sprung up, and about the
hour of sunset, our old friend, Eva, who had only the
day previous arrived in Ireland with the baronness and
her family, sought the village of Rossmore.

It was long past the time at which Eva had hoped
to reach the village, and she turned her steps immediately to the cottage in which she last left her grandfather and her aunt. Sad news, however, it was her
lot to hear; her aunt had died shortly after her departure from Ireland; the youth Bernard had been
sent to college through the benevolence of a gentleman
in the neighbouring town, and old Fitzgerald was now,

Eva was informed, perfectly imbecile; in fact, he was no longer master of his own actions; " Indeed, Miss Eva," continued the good woman, in whose cottage her grandfather had taken up his abode, " sure and it is a sight enough to move the hardest heart to see that poor old man; but here comes his Riverence, Miss," she added, as Father De Vere was seen in the distance, slowly walking up the lane which led to the groups of humble cottages by the roadside, his breviary in hand, " and the good Father will tell you better than I can do, of the strange way in which the old man now talks."

Pleased again to meet her old friend, but with the tears in her eyes at the melancholy narration, she had heard, Eva advanced to meet the Priest, who received her with a hearty welcome, such as Irish hearts so well know how to give; then his own benevolent-looking countenance grew sad, and placing his hand on Eva's shoulder, he said,—

" Pray to God to give you courage, my dear child, for I have bad news to tell you; your grandfather, Eva "—

" I have heard tidings of my family already, Father, from Mrs. Conolly; my poor aunt is dead, Bernard fortunately taken charge of, and my grandfather imbecile."

" Worse than imbecile, Eva; he is a prey to the most sad delusion; he goes daily to the old spot on which his happy home once stood; he fancies it is still his dwelling, but that it requires repairs and alterations, and that having lost his property in the failure of a bank, he will have to wait yet some few weeks before he can get it put in order; then he besets the carpenters far and near, desiring them to draw up estimates for the charge of repairs, and they, pitying his sorrowful and harmless state, humour his delusion. But it is a dreadful thing to see that aged man, whether the weather be hot or cold, wet or dry, no matter, he sallies forth immediately after hearing mass, and when he reaches a spot near what was once the gate of his happy home, he sits him down on a little hillock, draws forth pencil and paper, calculating the possible cost of rebuilding; and I have then watched and seen him after a while, lay down his pencil, muse with himself, and then burying his aged face within his hands, I have heard him exclaim, ' O, Mary, Mary, when will you and the boy return to me? how cruel of you to stay away so long;' then, when I have gone up to him and tried to rally him, he has exclaimed in the most earnest manner, ' Let me beg of you not to fail to tell me when you hear of the arrival of the next packet from Liverpool, as Mary is sure to return home by it;' nay, so strongly is he beset by this delusion, that he has often come to the Presbytery late at night, and early in the morning, to implore me not to forget his request, or to ask me if the packet has arrived, and if Mary be amongst the passengers."

" O, this is indeed dreadful, said Eva, bursting into tears, let me hasten to him at once; where may I find him?"

" At the old place, Eva; late as is the evening hour, there you are sure to meet him till the darkness of night veils the ruined homestead from his sight, there you will find poor Fitzgerald seated."

Eva was turning with a hasty step to the road which led to the spot where the farm had stood, when the Priest, as if a thought had suddenly occurred to him, said—

" Remember, Eva, I wish to see you very early in the morning; if possible, be with me immediately after mass."

Eva gave the required promise, and with a very heavy heart set out in search of her aged relative.

The sun had long set, but the night was beautifully clear, revealing every crystal drop from the late shower, which sparkled like a diamond on each shrub and flowret around.

Dimly in the fading light, there Eva could see a dark object bending forward, and she recognised her grandfather leaning on his stick, whilst before her lay the ruined house, the doors wrenched off their hinges, the roof torn off, save where here and there the thatch still clung to the walls, or hanging over them, waved to and fro in the night wind, whilst in the distance, frowning as it were on the sad quietude of the scene in the valley beneath, rose a chain of hills almost mountainous in their height, now veiled in the bluish mist which crept over them.

And Eva now stood beside the old man whose snow-white locks fell over his shoulders, and from whose lips ever and anon fell such words as these:—

"Yes, I think by the winter I shall be able to re-build this ruined place, but I must look well into those accounts, and call in all outstanding debts; then, heaving a deep sigh, he added, passing his hand across his forehead, and there is so much confusion here, my thoughts are so disconnected, nothing seems clear, and then Mary so long absent; then, after a pause, he continued, Mary, Mary, what has happened thee, my best darling, that your poor old father is left like this: then his head sunk upon his hand and Eva could hear his deep sob and saw that aged man was weeping as women only are wont to weep.

Eva stood beside him unnoticed, for he had not heard the sound of her light step in the thick grass; and now, dashing away the tears from her eyes and making a poor endeavour at a smile, she laid her hand on the old man's shoulder, and said,—

"Dear grandfather, your Eva has come to see you; but come, what do you do here so late, and the night dews falling so heavily?"

"Eva, Eva," half unconsciously murmured the old man, rising from the little hillock on which he had been seated with the support of his stick; and then, gazing in his grand daughter's face, he exclaimed, "why yes, it is Edmund's child; how glad I am to see you, Eva," he rambled on, leaning on the arm which she tendered him, "but see, it is not yet quite dark, and I must point out a few things to you before we go home. You see now, Eva, how sadly the old farm-house needs repair, so sadly, indeed, that I am obliged to sit here all day, and just have my meals and sleep at Mrs. Conolly's; the roof is gone, Eva, the place is a wilderness; and see how hard I have been at work," he added, drawing from his pocket a memorandum book full of calculations; "I find that it will take some hundreds to build it all up again, and I have hard work with the builders hereabouts to get anything like an estimate from them, so when Mary comes home, for she has been a long while absent, a long while from me now, well then I mean to go to Dublin and engage some of the best workmen to come and undertake the affair for me."

It was with difficulty that Eva could restrain her tears as the old man rambled on thus, but she thought it best to humour his delusion, and assenting to all his observations, replied, "I quite agree with what you say, but I think we had best return home, now, for we shall both suffer from this damp night air else."

"Home, child," he murmured, half in irritation, "this is my home, I never knew any other, I only have lodgings at Mrs. Conolly's; were it not for you, child, I should not leave this place yet, but I must not allow you to suffer on my account, so let it be as you will."

Slowly, then, they proceeded on their way to Dame Conolly's cottage, he ever and anon rambling on in the like manner, proving to Eva, beyond a doubt, that reason was banished from its throne.

The moon had now risen, and far as the eye could reach the country was bathed in its pale silvery light. On one side lay the ruined homestead, and here and there, scattered in various spots, the ruins of several humble cottages, while far in the distance rose the stately mansion of the Honble. Mr. Bishop, its white walls gleaming through the trees. Above were the blue heavens studded with innumerable stars, gleaming like diamonds in the firmament, whilst the pale moon sailing in silent majesty through the cloudless sky, shone full on the face of the aged man who leaned so heavily for support on the arm of his young companion.

And Eva looked up into the blue heavens above, and thought of the surpassing patience of God, who for his own wise ends was so long suffering, for on her arm leaned, like a helpless child, the man who despite his age was one short year since sound in mind and vigorous in body; there lay the ruined farm, beside her, that decrepid form with its poor distraught mind enshrined within, and yonder lay the proud estate of the author of all this mischief, the Honble. and Rev. Rector, and this, O parody on religion and good feeling, and charity, was all the work of this Christian Clergyman, this disgrace to his country, his profession, and the age in which he lives.

A few moments brought them to the cottage of Mrs. Conolly, in which without any difficulty Eva procured a bed for the night, and then, early on the following morning, after a sleepless and restless night, she hastened to her devotions in the little Chapel: after which she sought Father De Vere agreeably to his desire, little deeming that fresh ill news was in store for her.

After the first salutation was over, and Eva had expressed her sorrow at the state in which she had found her grandfather, the Priest, glancing at her mourning garments, enquired, if she were in mourning for her mother, and if so, did she know how the property had been disposed of?

Eva replied in the affirmative, adding,—

"I am utterly ignorant, Father, of the movements of my sisters and my step-father, and, indeed, I count every moment as an age till I meet them again; the Baron has travelled from place to place ever since I have been in his family, and consequently Dora's letters may have miscarried, though strange to say my own have remained unanswered; and, indeed, the last which I wrote was returned to me, from the Dead Letter Office, with the words, 'gone away, address not known,' on the envelope; and I frankly own the truth,

my mind is full of the most gloomy presentiments, .
I know no peace till I see my sisters once more."

Father De Vere was naturally a kind-hearted man,
and he was attached, moreover, to Eva with that
affection existing within the Church's pale, between
those who have brought the young to the baptismal
font, and then taught them the first truths of salvation,
and those, who in after years, are often heard to declare
that none have held to them the same place as that
first old friend, who watched over and guided the early
days of their youth.

Thus it was that the eyes of Father De Vere, became
humid as he took a copy of the *Times* newspaper from
a table beside him, and said to Eva, as he unfolded it,—

"I can give you news of those you love, Eva; but,
raise your heart to God for one moment, there is much
to try and test your patience, my child, but much to
be grateful for still; for you will see how God has
carried them through many trials to meet you again
unscathed."

Eva was the creature of impulse, and Father De
Vere knew it right well, and thus it was that she rose
as he spoke, and with a countenance pale as marble,
advanced to the table; for his words surely preluded
the announcement of some dire misfortune.

The Priest almost startled, glanced on that white
face, he noted the hand placed on the heart, in a vain
endeavour to still its tumultuous throbbing; and taking

her hand kindly within his own, he said, pointing to a paragraph in the paper,—

"Read this advertisement, Eva, my dear child; these girls *can* be none other than your own sisters."

The advertisement alluded to run as follows :—

"Should these words meet the eye of Bernard Fitzgerald, of Rossmore, Ireland; or of Miss Eva Fitzgerald, supposed to be at present either in St. Petersburgh or Vienna, residing as governess in the family of a German Baron, named Von Liebenstein; they are requested immediately to communicate with the Rev. Edward Lawrence, O.S.B., who has important information to disclose, relative to the sisters of the said Eva Fitzgerald."

The paper fell from the hands of the poor girl as she perused these lines; her countenance was deathlike in its hue, and she leaned for support on the chair of the Priest, murmuring,—

"Ah! blessed Mary, what new misfortune is in store for me? I must to England without delay."

"Courage, my child;" said the Priest, "God is merciful, and tries not his chosen ones above their strength, you have much trial to face, Eva, but trust me there will yet be a silver lining to the cloud; God will not forsake you."

"Pray for me, dear Father and best of friends," said Eva, as sinking on her knees she besought his blessing; and then with a heart in truth very sad, but full of high and holy resolves, this woman, young in years, but old in will and energy, sought the solitude of her chamber, to meditate for a few hours on what she should do, to think and pray, and *then* to execute.

CHAPTER XIII.

Eva's visit to S—— Poor-house.—The meeting with Catherine.
　—Various plans suggested as to the solving of that knotty
　point, how to get a living.

Two days later Eva again entered the little parlor of
Father De Vere, and in the short interval of time that
had elapsed, how much had our courageous heroine
accomplished.

The bright glow of health, which once was Eva's,
had vanished, and the girl looked haggard and worn in
the extreme; in fact her case was one of those in
which the health might be far more likely to give way
beneath the pressure of mental anxiety, than the
energetic mind or the indomitable persevering will, to
yield under any obstacle that might present itself.

Eva then advanced to meet her old friend, exclaiming,—

"I have come to bid you farewell, Father De Vere, my
grandfather and myself depart for London to-night."

"What are you thinking of, Eva," replied the Priest; "you know not, my dear child, the burthen you are taking on yourself; think well before you remove the poor old man, besides your situation you yet fill; what arrangements have you made with the Baroness Von Liebenstein."

"I was travelling the whole of yesterday in order to see my kind friend;" replied Eva, "they sympathise with me, have added a generous present to my salary, and promised to assist me with their purse, as soon as I have decided on what can be done for Kate and Dora, supposing our worst apprehensions are verified, and that the property has found its way into Morden's hands; whilst I am able to work," added Eva, "I cannot suffer my grandfather to continue, as I am certain he now is, a burthen on yourself; far from the scene of his former happiness, his mind may yet partially recover itself; and really, looking calmly into things, I do not see that there is any different course for me to pursue. I must hope for the best."

"No other course; no, not for one whose watchword is duty," said the Priest, half aloud, and forgetful for the moment of Eva's presence. Then addressing her, he said, "Fear not; you will have your reward, even here. And now tell me, when can I for the last time see my old friend?"

"When you please," replied Eva. "He is in high

spirits, for we shall pass through Liverpool, and he is firmly persuaded that he will see my poor Aunt Mary, when there." It was then arranged that Father de Vere should shortly visit Fitzgerald, at his customary haunt by the ruined house.

" Poor soul !" thought the Priest, " for a short time then you are happy, for one delusion followed closely on the heels of another in his poor demented brain, and he rambled on about little else but his meeting with Mary, and arrangements with London builders for the repairs of the old homestead."

And the farewell words were uttered, as Eva and the old man stood on the deck of the steamer which was to bear them to England; and Father De Vere remained as long as he could distinguish Eva and the old man, the former waving her white handkerchief in token of adieu.

In due course our travellers arrived in London, and fatigued as she was Eva waited not for repose, but leaving her grandfather in the care of the people at the inn, at which she had engaged rooms for the night, she hired a conveyance to take her to the residence of the Priest whose address was affixed to the advertisement.

Fortunately he was at home, and when the card bearing the name, " Eva Fitzgerald," was placed in his hand, and he eagerly advanced to meet her, exclaiming,—

"You have then seen my advertisement, this is most fortunate."

Eva could not speak; he saw her emotion, and he proceeded, delicately softening down the worst features of his story, but in two minutes she knew all; that they had been basely plundered of their inheritance, and were beggars on the face of the earth; one sister cast amongst strangers, the other an inmate of a Poorhouse.

"I must see Catherine at once," said the poor excited girl, pressing with affectionate gratitude the hand which Father Lawrence extended to her; "will you, Rev. Sir, direct me to the—the workhouse," she stammered forth, shrinking from uttering that word, to her so horrid.

"We will engage a cab, and I will myself go with you," said Father Lawrence, "but your sister is still very ill, I do not think you may remove her to-day."

Eva laid the very moments that elapsed under contribution as they accomplished the somewhat long journey; for so it appeared to her anxiously disturbed mind. At last they arrived at S—— Workhouse, and Eva sending in her card, was at once admitted with Father Lawrence to the matron's sitting-room.

With somewhat of an angry glance Mrs. Jennings greeted the good Priest, for she was not forgetful of last week's skirmish, and was at first inclined to demur at what she termed an unreasonable hour for Kate to

be seen, but the earnestness of Eva checked her; moreover, the demeanour of our heroine, her usual quiet
dignity of manner, which she had again recovered;
and even for vulgar minds are sure to scan everything
minutely, the simple elegance of her attire, all bespeaking
the refined lady, told on the heart of the matron.

"You had better come with me first, Mr. Lawrence,"
she said, addressing the Priest, "and prepare the young
lady's mind for seeing her sister; any little shock in
her present weak state will be bad."

To Eva, the few moments that elapsed seemed an age
in length, ere the matron returned to conduct her to
the room in which poor Catherine was still confined to
the bed, specially privileged; indeed, through the in-
strumentality of one of the guardians, a friend of the
matron, in having, humble though it was, this private
apartment destined for her use. The white-washed
walls and scanty furniture, however, struck a chill to
Eva's heart, as the matron led her to Catherine's bed,
near which stood Father Lawrence.

"My own Catherine!" "my dearest Eva," were the
ejaculations first heard by the Priest and the matron,
as the sisters fondly embraced each other once again,
and then Eva parted aside the long brown hair and
gazed sadly into the face of her favorite sister, and her
eyes filled with tears at the change she witnessed, for
the poor girl was fearfully altered.

The question then was mooted as to the time at

which Eva could remove her sister, and she was obliged unwillingly to own that it had best be referred to the doctor on the morrow.

Each, then, indulging a hope that on the following morning, when Eva agreed to call, that she might be suffered to remove her sister, they separated; Catherine enjoying a sweeter night's rest than she had known for some time past.

Ere she parted, too, with her new friend, Father Lawrence, he had called with her at a respectable house in which apartments were engaged for present use, and Eva then retraced her steps homeward.

Early the next day she proceeded to the workhouse, delighted enough to find that her proposal immediately to remove her sister was not considered imprudent, and then tendering her thanks to the matron, and handsomely feeing out of her little means both herself and the nurse who had attended on Catherine, she saw the latter placed once more beside her, and with a strange sensation at their hearts, the sisters gazed on the walls of the workhouse in which Catherine had for some months so strangely found a home. New cares, however, pressed heavily on Eva both as to mind and time; there was the imbecile grandfather, often querulous and impetuous in his temper, babbling still of his lost Mary and his ruined home, angrily demanding when he was to go back to the old place; then there was the loving and still suffering sister, too feeble yet even

to minister to her own wants, and there was uneasiness
as to Dora's well being; for, on Eva's applying at the
stately mansion, the address of which the matron had
given her, she had found, to her greater trial, that the
family, accompanied by Dora, were all in the country;
and, lastly, there was the never ending anxiety caused
by the reflection that without further delay employment
must be obtained or destitution be encountered. As
to Morden, he had evidently absconded, for all enquiries
had hitherto proved fruitless.

Now Eva had no one to consult as to the dreary
future which lay before her but her old kind friend the
parish Priest of Rossmore; her new friend, or rather
friends, the Benedictine Fathers, one of whom, Father
Lawrence had already so warmly interested himself in
Catherine's behalf, and the Baron and his wife, the
latter of whom, an Irish lady and heiress in her own
right, had become warmly attached to Eva during her
residence in her family.

As is always the case, contradictory advice was given,
for scarce two persons may be found to look at a thing
in the same light; and whilst the letter from Father
De Vere urged her to return to her situation, and this
from the purest of motives, because he considered her
own life would be a less anxious one, the Baroness
herself believed that her happiness would be best con-
sulted by bestowing on her the means to live with
those who so much needed her assistance. Accord-

ingly many plans were adopted only to be thrown aside, and it was at last decided, as amongst one of the very few things, that a gentlewoman might venture to turn to, that her chances of success might not be bad if in some one of the numerous suburbs around London a genteel light business could be established, and one for the sale of literature, combined with fancy goods, was finally selected. We had, however, forgotten to mention that Eva had received a letter from Dora which occasioned no small pain to both sisters; she spoke with enthusiasm of the life she led at Roseberry Hall, not, it appeared, in the capacity in which the girl had entered the family, but rather as the protegé and companion of Mrs. Bennett, descanting on the pleasant life she led and the luxuries around her; coolly, too, did she allude to the misfortunes of her grandfather and the death of her aunt, as also the severe illness of Catherine; but the greatest sting that Eva could have felt was couched in the few lines of the concluding paragraph, which told her that she had abjured the faith in which she was born.

Dora was vain and frivolous; her beauty was her bane, she was ready to listen to any who would flatter her; the matron, the sworn enemy of good Father Lawrence, had been the first to pour the poison into her ear; then to revile the faith whose practises, young as she was, she already deemed a too hard yoke; then came the fashionable luxurious wife of the rich citizen,

who, pleased with the naivete of the girl, and charmed
with her beauty, amused herself with it like some child
with a pretty toy, which, in the caprice of the moment,
she might hereafter throw carelessly aside. Of that,
more hereafter; for the present, Mrs. Bennett was well
pleased; moreover, had she not converted from the
errors of Rome the beautiful girl of whom she lately
had become so strangely acquainted, so that really
Dora felt herself something of a heroine; she was feted
everywhere, admired by all, and on the high road to
future misery.

CHAPTER XIV.

Going into business.—Large outlay and profits doubtful.—Customers decidedly in the minority.

PASS we over the next few months! untiring energy, industry, and exertion were not wanting; but this is all so common-place, and there was so little of incident in Eva's life, that as her biographer we find it all very dull, so shall merely speak, *en passant*, of some few of the difficulties she encountered; *au reste*, it would be well if young beginners with their spirits high and hearts full of hope, especially of the softer sex, were to remember which Eva, and many wiser than herself, fail to do, that success must be a work of time, even under the most flattering circumstances; that as Rome was not built in a day, so profits will not tell in equally with the daily wants of life, and that it is hard to hear the words *persevere*, *persevere*, for ever dinned into our wearied ear, when reason and common sense tell us

that where the returns cannot be obtained, and the
treasury begins to fail, perseverance is a myth which
cannot in any way be accomplished ; and so we will
pass lightly over the imbecility and delusions of old
Fitzgerald, which wore away as the constant dripping
of water wears away a stone, the patience of the still
feeble Catherine and sorely tried the affectionate Eva ;
the long weary hours when no one visited their really
smartly kept shop, the sick at heart feeling experienced
by these two young women, when, as week passed after
week and month after month, they would find on cast-
ing up accounts, that one sixpence, perhaps, was the
profit of the day.

The cold apathy with which they tried to listen when
they were told mayhap they sold too dear, though they
knew the smallest minimum of profit only would be
theirs, when night would come, and, too often, *nothing*
had been the order of the day.

Yet, though they nobly tried to school themselves
for that failure which a few months told them would
be inevitable, and tried to bear the disappointment
with equanimity ; though the stern world was all before them again, there were occasionally little occur-
rences which sorely tried the temper of Eva, in fact,
just as the angry element will sometimes beat to the
ground the stately tree and allow the young sapling of
the forest or wayside flower, to pass scatheless by ; so it
not unfrequently happens that those minds which can

calmly face a great misfortune and heroically brave an
imminent peril, yet bend oftimes beneath the daily
wearying discipline of life; and such minor evils as
these unfortunately set Eva's temper in a ferment,
under what she too truly termed the folly of some of
her lady patronesses. The suburb in which she lived
was poor, so far as the majority of its inhabitants were
concerned, but there were some well-to-do persons, and
amongst these were four rich ladies, the Misses Kildare,
who ever went on the *cheap system.*

One morning one of these ladies called to pay for a
neatly bound book; the paper was excellent, the type
was good, the engravings of the best and not a few in
number, and it was issued by one of the first firms in
London for the use of schools. Two shillings was the
price; but, to Eva's infinite amazement, two pence was
the sum laid down, and the lady exclaimed at the same
time with a smile—

" O, how good of that dear Father Hornby to get up
these books so cheap; only twopence, only think!"

"Twopence, madam," exclaimed Eva, "why reflect
for a moment and you will see it could not be; the
price of the book is two shillings!"

"Two shillings!" repeated the lady, "well, to be
sure, it *was* silly to think it was but twopence," and
placing the money in Eva's hand she left the shop.

" Catherine," said Eva, as she reentered the parlour,
" Miss Kildare must surely have taken it into her head

that Father Hornby has nothing else to do but *amuse* himself by compiling books, pay for printing them, and give them away gratuitously."

Another lady, a few days later, assured Catherine in Eva's absence, that lace prints, for which the large sum of a halfpenny was asked, had been sold to her four for a penny!

Then there was a Mr. Messent, who, on Eva's first location in the neighbourhood, had really seemed warmly to interest himself in behalf of her new effort; but,—ah, me!—there are some who immediately take offence if their advice be not scrupulously followed; and thus it was that Eva lost this gentleman's friendship; "Why not sell the serials of the day? she was surely wrong in passing them by; he would guarantee her success, let him see that she made the effort," &c.

But Eva and Kate knew that their very *small* means would not allow them to keep even a *very small* boy, and, as being of the softer sex, they could not *very* well hang about the offices of the cheap magazines themselves, they deemed it unwise to heed hints about penny serials, which gave great offence to Mr. Messent, who henceforth most cruelly deprived the ladies of his patronage, and never vouchsafed them a call hereafter.

Then, too, the sale of a book was such an anomaly, that it might be noticed, as it one day really was, in the following manner;—

"So, my dear Eva, you've sold a book," said a lady,

" I am very glad to hear that Miss Jones purchased one of you yesterday."

" Oh yes," replied Eva, much amused, " Miss Jones required something very cheap, so I sold her an eighteen penny book for a shilling."

And thus it was that in less than two years Eva was glad, with an aching heart, to throw up the whole concern; afterwards hearing, to her great astonishment, that it was said by several that she had not succeeded for want of tact, perseverance, &c., &c.; hearing which, she was wonderously inclined to quarrel with these simple souls; but remember, Eva, Rochefoucault has said, that misfortune is only another term for imprudence, so why grow angry, this is the way of the world.

And so it came to pass, that uncondemned by the only person whose opinion she need have cared for, the Baroness von Liebenstein, she accepted the offer that lady made her to return again into her family, and a few weeks later, bade adieu to her kind friends, the Benedictine Fathers, and two worthy warm-hearted persons with whom she had become acquainted, and returned to Ireland.

And what aching hearts had they not on leaving London; there was no hope to support them now; yet wait a while, Eva, for there may be still a silver lining to the cloud, which hangs so perseveringly over thy fortunes.

CHAPTER XV.

In which we meet again with Dora, who commits a sad faux pas, by frankly expressing her opinions on certain delinquencies of the Rector.

EVA little thought how near she was to Dora, when, a few days after her return, she arrived at Rossmore, with the intention of placing her grandfather again in the charge of Mrs. Conolly, designing to pay for his board out of her salary, whilst it was agreed that Kate should for the present assist in a conventual school in Dublin.

It was a lovely September evening, and the Rev. Mr. Bishop had invited a large party to the Rectory to celebrate the twenty-first birth-day of his son, and who should there be amongst the guests but Mr. and Mrs. Bennett, with their protegée, Dora, for Dora was just now in high request, she being a recent convert to the Protestant faith; then again, too, there was a noble guest present in the person of Lord Rathmore, an excellent and accomplished man, who, a firm adherent of Protestanism and of decidedly High Church principles, would yet never yield nor suffer any injustice to be perpetrated on his Catholic tenantry.

The Misses Bishop, who were old friends of the Bennetts, little deemed that in the beautiful girl whom their friend had converted to Protestantism they were about to meet with the sister of Eva, and there being not the slightest similarity between them, the farewells would doubtless have been spoken but for an unfortunate remark on the part of Dora herself.

It will readily be conceived on account of Dora's youth, and also her dependent situation in the family of Mrs. Bennett, that the girl owed her invitation into company so select as that now assembled in the Rector's mansion, solely to the fact of her apostacy from the Catholic faith; this she herself well knew, and vain and frivolous as she was, she liked the *prestige* attendant on her introduction into higher circles, though at the same time there was a canker worm which was gnawing at her heart, even when she appeared the gayest; for Dora had not thrown aside her faith for any motive save that of worldly gain.

Now, standing at one of the windows of the room in which the guests were assembled, she said to the astonished Miss Deborah—

"Are we not near to Rossmore? My grandfather held a large farm there, but he was a Catholic, and has been evicted with great cruelty by his landlord, who is the Rector of the place; so my sister Eva writes."

Miss Deborah stared in unfeigned astonishment on the fair speaker, and then exclaimed aloud to her father, who stood side by side with Lord Rathmore, "Why papa, do you know that our guest, Miss Fitzgerald, is positively sister to that Miss Eva who offended you so much, and grand-daughter to that poor half-witted old man, Fitzgerald, one of the evicted tenantry."

The Rector had not overheard Dora's unlucky speech about his cruelty, and now approaching with one of his blandest smiles, he exclaimed—

"How glad am I to know then that one of your family have received the light of truth; I found your sister, Eva, inflexible in her own evil ways, your grand-father a stern uncompromising bigot."

For a moment the early days of her innocent girl-hood, and Eva's affection, glanced before the mind of Dora. She flushed to her very temples, with, for the moment, a righteous indignation, and exclaimed—

"My sister, Rev. Sir, will ever be firm in her adherence to the Catholic faith; my grandfather I have always heard spoken of as being a good and upright man, but as one who has been hardly and cruelly dealt with. I have heard that he has become imbecile; nay, that he is now insane through his eviction from his farm."

"Are you aware, young lady, when you animadvert

in such strong terms on your relative's eviction, that I was his landlord, and that it was because he was too stubborn minded to allow his grandchild to receive the pure light of gospel truth that it was considered necessary to make an example of one who was enough above his fellows to become, as it were, an example for them to follow," said the Rector.

If Dora was vain and frivolous, she was no less haughty; she had bartered her faith for the favor of those amongst whom she now moved from a desire of gratifying her vanity and escaping from the poverty in which her sisters were plunged; still, like an oasis in the desert, there was one green spot in Dora's heart, she was not so irretrievably bad but that she could feel some little for the sufferings of her own kinsfolk, and having, without knowing she was in the very house of her grandfather's oppressor, allowed the words we have repeated to fall from her lips, as also the expression of her own feelings, she was not the girl to recall them or flinch from any disagreement which those words might occasion; Dora saw, too, more than one glance wrathfully levelled on her countenance, her spirit chafed under what she considered personal rudeness, and nothing loth to enter the lists now that her self-love was wounded, she replied—

"Indeed, Rev. Sir, I did *not* know that you were the gentleman Eva has written of so indignantly; had I known it I should not have been guilty of such a mis-

take as to give such expression to my own feelings as I
have unwittingly done; *having* done so I cannot recall
my words, and with regard to Eva who has so angered
you, I must add, that had *she* thrown off her faith as I
have done or my aged grandfather, *they* would have
been ornaments to their new religion such as I shall
never be; for as to Eva, she is a model of affection
and self denial."

A murmur ran round the room as Dora unheeding
in her haughty anger the consequences that might
accrue spoke thus; the spirit of her dead mother was
within her, her clear fair complexion was flushed with
· irritation, and her full dark eye flashed indignantly as
she spoke, yet there was comfort for her too, for a voice
at the further end of the apartment, apparently issuing
from a table where a knot of gentlemen had a few moments before been discussing some political questions,
exclaimed in a loud tone—'

"Well said, Dora, Eva is too good to barter her
faith for the favor of man; her grandsire, too, holds it
far too highly, and there is yet hope for *you*, who have
given utterance to such sentiments."

For a moment every eye was turned to the spot
whence the voice had proceeded, surely it was one of
those gentlemen, who nevertheless seemed not to have
noticed Dora, who stood angry and flushed in the midst
of that little group; but no, each one stoutly asserted
that he had not even noticed, much less borne any part

in what had been taking place, and the Rector's thoughts now carried him back to a certain memorable evening, when, by a circumstance similar to the above, discord had reigned amongst his guests, for the reader will not have forgotten the scene which followed the evictions when the Rector met his friends in his own mansion in the evening of the day on which they had taken place.

But still more discomforted did he feel when the good Lord Rathmore approached the girl, and said,—

"I have heard something of your family history, Miss Fitzgerald, from dear friends of my own, the Baron Von Liebenstein and his excellent wife, and I have met your sister Eva in their family; the story of your conversion to our faith has deeply pained those who love you, for myself, I like not these so-called conversions in persons so young; but you know best the motives which have led you on, I do not; but I heartily unite in the wisdom of a remark already made, implying that if an error has been committed, there is still virtue enough left to retrieve the past; I have heard, too, of your old grandfather, and it is my intention to see him on the morrow."

Mrs. Bennett had really thought the senses of her *protegée* had almost abandoned her, so amazed was she, that she, whom she had patronized with her gracious protection, and snatched from so much misery, should have dared forget herself so far, as to speak as

she had done; and she was on the point of ordering
Dora to withdraw from the room, when the courtly
Lord Rathmore approached her.   Now, Mrs. Bennett
was one of the veriest hangers-on in fashionable circles ;
by dint of her husband's wealth, she never failed by
any means, how unworthy soever they might be, to
obtrude her company on persons of a class above her
own; and partly through the forbearance and good
nature of the *exclusives*, amongst whom she intruded
herself; partly through her own tact, her apparently
ladylike demeanour, and an indomitable resolution,
never to take offence; Mrs. Bennett could boast the
entree of many a Belgravian mansion.   Thus it was
then that the severe rebuke she was about to administer
to Dora, died on her lips ; and this veritable toadeater
was already planning in her own mind, divers little
schemes to be put in practice, by which she might
hope to push her way, even into acquaintanceship with
Lady Rathmore, and eventually, (who would venture
to say that it might not be, in this world of wonders),
secure a fashionable alliance with his Lordship's
family, for one of her own grown-up children.

The pleasure of the evening had, however, been
marvellously disturbed by the very unlooked for *con-
tretemps* which had taken place; and sundry speeches
were made by the Rector's family and three of his own
party, not very flattering either to Dora, or her protectress for the time being, some few of which found

their way, as it was amiably determined they should do, to the hearing of these persons; and luckily for Dora, as Mrs. Bennett had her own part to play, she escaped any severe reprimand, but merely a whispered caution to be careful how she gave expression to her feelings in any mixed company, and then drawing Dora's arm within her own, with a profound obeisance to Lord Rathmore, the little woman, full of ideas of self-importance, sailed majestically out of the room.

CHAPTER XVI.

The lamp of life slowly expires within sight of the ruined
homestead.—The Rector steps upon the scene in time to
survey the twofold ruin he has caused : viz., the crumbling
ruin—the work of man's hands, and the wreck of the
immortal mind.

THE excellent Lord Rathmore had heard much in his
occasional visits at the Baron's residence, to make his
faith in the virtue of an old friend waver somewhat in
its strength ; and being one of those persons who so
rightly pause ere they pronounce judgment, he had
determined to go and personally investigate the state
of affairs at Rossmore, ere he could make up his mind
that a Christian minister, himself rich, too, in worldly
wealth, and also sprung from his own class, could have
so strangely forgotten himself, as with crowbar and
pickaxe to authorise the demolition of his tenants'
property; and that, too, on a point which spoke ill for
the tolerant spirit of the Rev. Gentleman.

It was with no very pleasant feelings that the Rector heard his noble guest avow his intention of visiting Rossmore on the following day; and almost his first thoughts were of the good nobleman, when he arose on the following morning.

The heavy mist of an October morning had cleared away as the day advanced, and furnished with the address he had obtained from Eva, Lord Rathmore, followed by a groom, rode over to the village of Rossmore, which was situated some fifteen miles from his own residence.

Eva was herself at the cottage of the worthy Mrs. Conolly, who had promised to keep a strict watch on the movements of the old man, who had latterly fallen into so sad a state as to need the exercise of no small watchfulness in his regard.

It was somewhat past mid-day ere Lord Rathmore arrived at the cottage, but the object of his search was not there, he had been, Mrs. Conolly informed Eva and himself, unusually restless, and even while a heavy fog enveloped the surrounding country in obscurity, had determined on going to his accustomed haunt, his ruined home.

Thither, then, Lord Rathmore determined on accompanying Eva, and a walk of some twenty minutes brought them to the accustomed spot.

The foliage of the trees now bore the bright and varied tints of Autumn, and beneath the feet lay the

K

sere and withered leaves, telling of the death of the year; afar to the right was a range of mountains, their summits scarcely discernible in the mist, which still overhung them; here along the route which Eva and her noble companion pursued, stood the ruins of some humble cottage, which had been inhabited by some poor cotter; there a low roofed building, on which was painted the words, "Irish Mission Schools;" and afar, a little to the left, in a pleasant glade in which the noonday sun glinted merrily down, as if in mockery of the waste of desolation around; lay the ruins of a dwelling-house, which had evidently belonged to one of the superior class of farmers.

Far and wide around lay several acres of richly cultivated land, which had evidently had many long years of care and pain bestowed on it, to rescue it from the waste bog which surrounded it; whilst the ruined dwelling-house still bore tokens of its having once been a comfortable and happy home, the abode, indeed, of the once opulent farmer, Eva's grandsire.

"My Lord," said Eva with much emotion, as she pointed to the ruined building, "that ruin was once my dear grandfather's homestead; see, it has been levelled with the earth, because at the bidding of the merciless Mr. Bishop, he would not barter my cousin Bernard's faith; these smiling fields, rich in produce, were cultivated by his own hands for more than forty years; now, a stranger reaps the harvest he has sown; and see, my Lord, there sitting in the old place is my venerable relative, ever at his work, gazing on the old place, making his calculations, poor old man," added Eva, " 'tis well, perhaps, so sweet a delusion is thine."

The two softly approached the old man, who, with paper and pencil in hand, seemed bending over his task. " He does not hear our footsteps," whispered Eva, as she now stood almost by his side.

The Earl glanced over his shoulder and saw the figures roughly sketched in the paper Fitzgerald held ; Eva laid her hand upon his shoulder, exclaiming—

"Dear grandfather, why do you sit here on this damp grass, this cold October day; see, Eva has come to you again, let me lead you from this place."

Eva met with no reply; hastily, as if a sudden fear had fastened on her heart, she darted forwards ; one moment she gazed on that aged face, the next she clasped her hands together, and passionately exclaimed "Ah! my Lord, what new woe is this; Oh, tell me, can this be death ?"

Much shocked, the Earl supported the sinking Eva, and gazed in the face of Fitzgerald. Ah, yes, the unmistakeable impress of death was there, its grey shadow had flitted some three hours since over that venerable countenance, the dark grey eye was fixed, the hand which still tightly clasped the pencil and the paper was cold and stiff, the features rigid and immoveable.

"But see," says Eva. "Ah, my Lord! his last
thoughts were of peace and love, and full of faith he
died conscious that his spirit was parting from this
earth, for behold his right hand, half within the folds
of his vest, clasps a small silver crucifix. Yet, O my
God, alone his parting spirit went forth," added Eva,
bursting into tears and throwing herself on her knees
beside the corpse, she madly pressed those hands
long cold in death.

"Eva Fitzgerald," exclaimed the Earl, this is a
dreadful sight; stay here awhile whilst I go in quest of
assistance; summon religion to your aid, and bless God
that he has been removed; one moment," he added, "two
ladies are advancing, they will procure help for us; but
see, Eva, continued the Earl, surely you should know
one of them better than myself, for does not your sister
approach?"

Immediately Eva started back as Dora advanced in
all the pride of her youth and beauty. Eva remembered her heartlessness, remembered her apostacy, but
Dora heeded not that gesture of coldness, she would
not be repulsed, but murmuring the words "Eva, forget the past," pressed her to her heart, and then took
her place beside the corpse of the old man.

But other and still more unwilling eyes were to gaze
on that rigid and immoveable countenance; a gay
party now approach; a gentleman and two ladies, the
latter laughing and talking merrily, for the cares of life

have not troubled them over much yet; but as they advance nearer they immediately pause, and one of the ladies exclaimed, " Why surely it cannot be—but yes—it *is* Lord Rathmore."

Lord Rathmore heard and knew the voice ; he turned and gazed on the party ; his just and noble soul full of indignation that such doings should be perpetrated by a Christian minister in a Christian land ; then advancing he coldly touched the hand of the Rector, for he it was who accompanied his daughters on their morning stroll, and drawing him somewhat nearer to the spot, he said in a low voice, " Look, Mr. Bishop, yonder is poor Fitzgerald ; God has at last called him to his rest, neither you nor any mortal man can harm him more ; but not for the uncounted wealth of worlds would I have to answer for that morning's work of yours, when, in the name of religion, or rather, should I say, of a bigotted intolerance, *you*, a minister of my own Church, levelled to the earth the home of that aged man, and turned *him* and *his* wanderers on the world."

The scene on which he gazed explained the whole ; the Rector said not a word, but stiffly bowing to his former friend, turned with his daughters hurriedly from the spot.

CHAPTER XVII.

The march of intellect.—Modern education.—Prodigies of learning and accomplishment in the rising generation.

THE year is now on the wane, for many weeks have passed since Eva laid her grand-sire in the village church-yard at Rossmore; and deeply as she felt the death of the old man, she could not but own that his release was a happy one. So melancholy, too, was the aberration which had unsettled his once strong mind, as to make it really a pitiable thing to watch him under the many different phases which it assumed; and, undoubtedly, had his life been prolonged, Eva must have incurred both the pain and the expense of putting him under restraint.

Dora continued still at Mrs. Bennett's, though not

on quite the same terms as formerly, for the lady had a keen suspicion that her own son wished to marry the beautiful but portionless girl whom she had patronised indeed, but certainly had not the faintest desire that Dora should become her daughter-in-law.

Catherine still remains at the Convent, and vague ideas at present float through her mind that she would like to bid farewell to a world in which she has already seen much sorrow, and vague as are those ideas, there is a great probability that they will one day assume a more tangible shape, and that the gentle Catherine may wear the habit of a Sister of Charity.

Eva resides still in the family of the German Baron and his amiable Irish lady. In the spring of the following year they talk of returning to Vienna, and of Eva accompanying them; but of this more anon, for Eva will, ere long, be the hospitable mistress of a true Highland home.

It wanted one short week of Christmas-day when a happy party composed of the Baron Von Liebenstein and his wife, Colonel Monteith, and Eva, drove up the avenue leading to a noble mansion in South Devon: the extreme mildness of its winters had led Lord Rossmore to purchase a small estate in this spot, and thither he had invited his friends to spend the festive season of Christmas.

Eva was charmed with the glorious scenery around her, in which hill and dale, wood and water, all bore a conspicuous part, and as the carriage emerged from a noble avenue, a burst of admiration escaped her lips.

The gently undulating ground, covered with the greenest verdure, swept away to the borders of a lake whose clear blue waters rippled beneath the rays of the December sun ; beyond, far as the eye could reach, rose a range of hills, whilst here and there, dotted between the trees, were the white villas of the neighbouring gentry, and above, on a rising ground, stood the light and elegant mansion of Lord Rathmore, its style of architecture closely resembling that of an Italian palace rather than a villa in our cold northern clime.

Eva's lot had been singularly fortunate in so far that she had met with warm friends ; but there was an under current of which she was little aware, and it will be seen hereafter how she came to be included, a portionless dependent as she was, in the invitation Lord Rathmore had given to his friends.

A really intellectual circle was that which met at the Earl's residence to celebrate the Christmas festivities, and the Baroness laughingly remarked to Eva on the second day of their visit, that really there was but one thing wanting to make the estate complete in its arrangements, and this was a Catholic chapel ; but the good Earl was out of the Church's pale, so Christmas, as kept in the olden time with Catholic associations, could not be had at Woodlands, so perforce Catholic rites must be looked for elsewhere.

Each day, too, did the Earl arrange his plans so that time should not hang heavy on the hands of his friends, and the hours flew away rapidly as they are wont to do with those whose hearts are light, on whom there is no present care, who see around them all the appliances of wealth and high position, and who, looking on the world beyond, so fraught with misery and sorrow to the majority, have virtue enough to raise their hearts in thankfulness to God for the blessings they enjoy, and thus acknowledging the benefit, there naturally springs forth benevolence to those less fortunate than themselves.

It wanted but a few days of the time appropriated for the return of the party to Ireland, when one morning Eva was surprised by a sudden exclamation on the part of the Baroness, who had been conning over the list published in the daily *Times* of those united for better for worse, as time should show.

"Is it possible, Eva," she exclaimed, "that your sister Dora has positively become Mrs. Edward Bennett: yet here, read the announcement of her wedding," she continued, placing the paper in the hands of the astonished Eva, and pointing to the paragraph in question.

Yes, indeed it was true; Dora had calculated her chance for this world at all events, for thus ran the announcement:—

"On the 11th inst. at St. George's, Hanover Square, Edward Bennett, Esq. to Dora Fitzgerald."

The paper dropped from Eva's hands; she sat for a moment or two lost in thought, and then said—

"Dora was not happy when I last saw her, she has stepped as it were clandestinely into Mr. Bennett's family, and has bartered her faith for gold."

She was still musing over the occurrence when Lord Rathmore entered, and laughingly enquired if they would like to accompany him to a certain public school established for the children of the working classes, not a mile distant from Woodlands, which he had been urged to visit as the only person of influence in the neighbourhood, and the gentleman who begged his attendance and who was himself a great man, foremost in all educational movements, assured the Earl that he really would feel quite delighted at the astonishing progress which the boys were making in education.

Madame Von Liebenstein assented; and Eva and herself being joined by the Colonel and the Baron, Lord and Lady Rathmore led the way by a short cut through the fields to the school in question.

But ere they entered the building set apart for the boys, Lady Rathmore suggested that they should inspect the girls' school, adding, "Really I never felt a greater disgust than that which I experienced the other

day: a young lady whose family has undergone a reverse of circumstances, and who is known to the Earl
and myself as being an accomplished and clever girl,
yet failed after long trial to obtain a situation as governess, overstocked as the market unhappily is, in the
unfortunate dearth of employment for ladies; much to
the mortification of her friends and to the surprise of
myself and the Earl," added Lady Rathmore, "she offered
herself to pass the examination for a Queen's scholar-
ship; a lady in the strictest sense of the word is Lucy
Vernon, and an accomplished one too; yet, will you
believe it, Madame, she failed to obtain a vacant ap-
pointment because she could not answer one of the
difficult questions proposed, and which, nevertheless,
was answered, by a girl in very humble life, some time
a pupil-teacher in the school; but here we are," added
her ladyship, "come in and see for yourselves."

"And these are the girls who will become the wives
of the laboring classes, the mothers of the rising generation," said Madame, as in company with her friend
she left the building to join her husband, who, with
the Earl and Colonel Monteith, had gone to the boys'
school. "Can we longer wonder that under this absurd
system the English housewife as she was in days of
yore no longer exists, that society is turned topsy-turvy,
that the lower class are seeking to fill the ranks of the
middling class; that instead of being content to be
upper servants, they must, forsooth, be governesses;

and that few of the workmen's wives can make dresses
for themselves or clothes for their children.   Shades of
our grandmothers and great grand-dames look out of
your graves and marvel at the change."

It was with much difficulty that Eva repressed her
risible faculties when on entering the school-house she
beheld the Earl and the Colonel standing amidst a
knot of boys to whom the master was propounding
questions which we much suspect, had they been addressed either to the gallant Colonel or his noble friend,
neither would have been able very readily to answer.
Eva understood short-hand, and drawing forth her
tablets which had been in request when listening to the
questions and answers put to the girls, she wrote the
following now propounded to a boy who looked like the
son of some agricultural labourer.

*In three proportional lines, what proportion will the
parallellogram made by the first and third bear to the
square of the second?*

The parallellogram and square are equal, replied the
boy.

" Will your lordship be good enough to question the
boys ?" said the Dominie, advancing to the Earl. " By
Jove," whispered Lord Rathmore in the ear of the
Colonel, " I could not ask the urchins a question for the
life of me;" then rising, he exclaimed, " I have not
much time, but I will hear the boys read."

" Capital,—well out of that," muttered the Colonel

to himself, and advancing to the door as if in fear lest
he should meet with any difficulty, for the head of the
gallant son of Mars was less full of knowledge than
those of the boys who stood in all their poverty before
him, he hastened away.

"Disgusting! is it not, Madame," said Lady Rathmore to the Baroness, as soon as they had fairly got
out of the precincts of the schools. "Is it any longer
matter for surprise that our domestic servants are
above their duties, or that the humble homes of our
poor cottagers are so shamefully mismanaged; that
their wives and daughters are, with this foolish system
of education, so carried out of their natural sphere,
that they positively will soon be above keeping their
little homes in order; and, at the present moment, indeed, very few of them know how to use their needles."

"Well said, Madame. I assure your ladyship I
never was more astonished than a few days since;
when, on looking over the numerous advertisements
in the daily *Times*, that great vehicle for requirements,
my eye fell on an advertisement to the effect that two
ladies were required to give their services in the cause
of education, partly in a charitable way, in an English
village; that they must have a small income, as only a
cottage, rent free, would be given them; but that their
drawing and music must be *of a superior kind*, as it
was to be introduced into the cottages of the humbler
classes. Well, certainly, I thought, as I read this

most ridiculous announcement, we shall, ere long, seek in vain for domestic servants, for they will soon become as accomplished, or even more so than their mistresses, and will look somewhat higher than household service.*
But, by the way, I know of a circumstance which bears very much on the subject of our conversation," added the Baroness, " and I will mention it to you."

" A few years since, a charitable Catholic lady, who had done much good in a village near Carmarthen, a foreigner herself, and the wife of a Protestant, Colonel Croft by name, sent to a young friend of mine,

---

* " The schools themselves by a too ambitious course of instruction, often tend to raise girls above domestic service, while imperfectly fitting them for it. The Rev. G. W. Procter of Devonport, in a communication made by him, refers at some length to the pupil-teacher system, acknowledging it to be a great improvement on the monitorial system, but strongly objecting to thus tempting and stimulating girls in humble life to endeavour to attain the power of answering such difficult questions as have been proposed at the examination for Queen's scholarships; saying, that it furnishes them with an excuse for shirking common sense every-day domestic duties, and fosters the idea of becoming the lady of the family; stating that respectable Christian mothers of humble life who would wish their daughters to live a modest, virtuous, useful life of humble industry, complain that the present system of female education is placing new and unlooked for difficulties in their way, making young girls impatient and dissatisfied with home restraints and home circumstances."—*The Times, September* 20, 1861.

a girl some ten or twelve years of age; this girl's father had been a laboring man, who had deserted his family, leaving his wife and four children chargeable to the parish; to prevent the loss of their faith, Mrs. Croft took the eldest, a boy of sixteen, to be her ostler, the second boy she also found employment for in her own house, one little girl she placed with a Sisterhood of Nuns at Newport, the other she sent to the care of my friend, herself a poor lady, struggling with the world, and keenly alive, for she had experienced it in her own family, to the difficulty of securing the blessing of a liberal education to those in her own position; well, this child, with its heavy unintellectual countenance, and its unkempt and unclean locks of fiery red hair, was received by my friend, Agatha Selwyn, as a most unwelcome charge, till preparations could be made in a certain Orphanage near London to receive her; and in progress of time the charity of a high dignitary in the Church, guaranteed the yearly sum to be paid for its reception; well, Lady Rathmore," continued the Baroness, "my friend, was quite correct in saying that the poorer classes now possess advantages, as far as education is concerned, of which the middle class are too often deprived; this child, whom no education could divest of coarse manners and positive vulgarity, whom mere accomplishment never could refine, had not only a common sound English education imparted to her, such as in after life would have proved a blessing, but

was taught to speak French; and called, three years
later, on Miss Selwyn, exulting in the very accomplishment that carried her out of her proper path in
life; while—said my friend, with a bitter sigh—we know
of many a wretched young lady whose efforts in the
cause of tuition are much impeded, because perchance
her struggling parents of gentle birth, cannot procure
her a like advantage."

As the Baroness made this remark, the little party
arrived at Woodlands; and many a hearty laugh was
indulged in during the remainder of the day, by the
Earl and the Colonel, at the idea of the haste with
which the latter had wended his way from the School-
house, lest a question should be propounded which he
could not answer.

CHAPTER XVIII.

Showing how the piety of the Rev. Mr. Bishop's hangers-on evidences itself in the demolition of Church windows.— The Veil of the Cloister and the Bridal Ring, are both in perspective.

On the fifth day of the new year, Eva and her friends bade farewell to their noble and hospitable entertainers, and retraced their steps to Dublin. Meanwhile, two letters had reached our heroine's hands, the perusal of which filled her with very different emotions. One was from Catherine, always good and gentle, telling how she by one of those providential circumstances, which we are too prone to call a fortuitous chance, had met at the Convent with her deceased mother's early friend, the amiable Miss Fortescue, whom we alluded to in an earlier part of our tale ; this lady's aged mother was now dead, and she was making a tour through Ireland, when on stopping at the Convent, in which Kate had found a temporary home, to make enquiries for a young attendant, she to her great surprise recognised, in the delicate girl presented to her by the Mother Superior, the daughter of her former humble friend, Ellen.

"But Catherine's wish was to take the Veil of a Sister of Charity, if it might ever be so;" she remarked half hesitatingly, in answer to Miss Fortescue's remark concerning her future prospects, and the elder lady smilingly replied,—

"Of that there is little doubt, Kate, provided you have the necessary vocation; however, I have a friend who is a Mother Superior of one of our London houses: my old friendship for your unhappy mother would, apart from weightier considerations, induce me to help you to accomplish such an object, therefore, I will be responsible for the necessary sum that will be required."

It may readily be imagined that Kate lost no time in communicating the news to Eva; ending her letter by stating, that she had since heard, that arrangements had been made for her almost immediate reception into the London Convent.

Dora's letter was at the same time, if we may so speak, written in a sad yet triumphant strain, for whilst a bitter spirit of melancholy and dejection seemed to overhang the writer, yet, there was a proud defiant air of exultation; too plainly saying, as clearly as if Dora's own lips had uttered the words, "I have gained what I have striven for: I have youth and health and wealth, and now I shall try my very best to

feel as happy as the thoughtless world takes me to be."
But it was all hollowness, all self-delusion, the last few
lines told this, in which Dora spoke with a bitter feeling of
wounded pride, at what she termed the impertinence
of her mother-in-law, who, forsooth, she added, refuses
to recognise my marriage with her son, because I
happened to have no fortune.

Was this then the end of Dora's hopes? we shall see:
she had lost her faith, had married a Protestant, and
against the wish of his family. "What will come
next," sighed Eva, as she put aside the letters, and
turned her steps to the village of Rossmore.

But there had been warm work in the usually
peaceful village; for see, the windows of St. Marie's
Church are smashed, as also several in the little Presbytery; and Eva found her apprehensions but too
correct; there had been a riot in the once peaceful
village; the population, fearfully excited, had at last
risen one against the other, Bible-readers, and Soupers,
and Catholics, formed themselves into thoroughly hostile
ranks; and who, amongst the whole crew of fanatics,
had first raised the passions of the people, and labored
harder than that veritable Pat Brennan, with whom
we made acquaintance in the Rector's Mission School?
yes, the apostate Catholic was infinitely the worst
amongst the evil-minded set, who for several months
past had been exciting the passions of the multitude,
none more audacious in their villany, none more

violent in their constant acts of daring outrage on the persons and property of the poor Catholic peasantry around; than was this wretched being, this excellent convert of Mr. Bishop and his family?

With deep sorrow Eva gazed on the evident signs of riot and disorder around, and a sigh escaped her as she paused on her way to the little Presbytery, and for a moment stood musing against one of the window frames, now denuded of the richly stained glass which it had once boasted.

"The Rev. Mr. Bishop's myrmidons have evidently been at work here, Miss Fitzgerald," said a well-known voice, and Colonel Monteith approaching offered her his arm to the Presbytery; on arriving at which they were met by Father De Vere, from whom they found that their surmises had been but too correct; that the intention of a band of rioters, which had gathered together a few nights since, had evidently been, not only to demolish the windows, but the entire building, had they not been checked in their work of destruction by the arm of the law; and that foremost amongst them was the Rector's *protegé*, the ex-Catholic, Patrick Brennan.

"But how came *you* here, Colonel?" said Eva, after the Priest had concluded his sad narration; "I little thought it was your intention to leave Florence Court to-day, and the time so speedily approaching for Herr von Liebenstein's return to Vienna."

"Principally on your own account, Mistress Eva, and from a wish to enlist your Reverend friend in my behalf," replied the Colonel. "Briefly then, Father De Vere," he continued, "I wish to transplant to my colder northern home in the Highlands of Scotland, a certain fair daughter of Erin; albeit, she may also be termed an English rose; still, I think the Emerald Isle may more fairly claim her for its own, for was she not born in this poor village of Rossmore; and are not your heart's best affections, my Eva, intertwined with those of old and faithful Ireland? Give me then a word, Father De Vere, and your blessing, if Eva frowns not on my suit, to my Irish bride and myself."

Eva spoke not a word, but her blue eyes filled with tears, and her hand trembled as she yielded it to that of the Priest, who placed it within the grasp of the Colonel, and his hearty, "God speed and bless you both," whilst his hand was placed on Eva's head, betrayed his emotion, for his voice shook as he uttered those few words.

To know Colonel Monteith was to esteem him, and Eva had known him long; but unendowed and dependent as she was, timid, modest and retiring, Eva dreamed not of aught but a return to Vienna, as the simple *protegée* of her high-born Irish friend, and the governess of her children.

"Time presses, Father De Vere," said the Colonel, for I must join my regiment shortly, and I wish my

Eva to be made acquainted first with our·Scottish home and friends; though Herr von Leibenstein and his lady have some time known my intentions, and will make all necessary arrangements for the wedding at their own residence; have you, my Eva, anything to suggest? for with the Church's blessing on our heads, I shall not tarry long."

"Yes I have," said Eva, smiling; "it is that Father De Vere leave for a short time his village home, and ——"

"And having baptized thee in thy infancy, unite thee at the altar," interrupted the Priest; "be it so, I will perform the ceremony with much pleasure."

It was then arranged that Father De Vere should proceed to Dublin early in the following month; and first leaving a handsome douceur with the Priest to repair in some degree the demolition of the Church, the worthy Colonel took his leave; rallying the now somewhat pensive Eva, who could with difficulty imagine that she who had risen that morning a poor dependent, was destined so shortly to become the bride of one whom she had long esteemed, though she did not dare to love; who was the heir to large landed property in the beautiful Isle of Skye, and equally estimable as a good Catholic Convert and a gallant soldier.

CHAPTER XIX.

Eva's visit to Dora.—An unhappy marriage.—The last grace is
bestowed but is cast carelessly aside.—Dora visits the ruins
of St. Kilda's Chapel.—The ramble to the cliff.

THREE years have passed away, Eva has long been a
happy wife, and far away from her own green Isle has
won the hearts of her husband's Scotch relatives and
the peasantry around by her unaffected piety and worth.
Catherine has been vested with the robes of a Sister of
Charity, and the sisters meet but rarely. Dora she
has never seen, but at last she has received a letter to
say that her husband has purchased an estate not far
from Skye, chiefly on account of the shooting, and
that it is her intention to proceed thither in order to
see Eva.

The wished for day at length arrived, but Eva found
her painfully altered, and could scarce believe that the
dignified woman, now in the full maturity of beauty,
who advanced to meet her, was the impulsive Dora of

earlier years. An air of cold constraint seemed to
hang over her; that pale proud face appeared as if it
was rarely lit up by a smile; her very attire, too, was
in harmony with the character she seemed to have
adopted; elegantly neat, yet at the same time most ex-
pensive, mused Eva, as Dora's youthful yet stately form,
robed in heavy black velvet, moved with the dignity of
an empress, across her no less stately apartments.

"Can this be a young wife and mother, thought
Eva; those garments are not suited to her age, that air
of repellant coldness, it betokens anything but happiness;" then, languidly taking a beautiful child from the
arms of its nurse, she listened to the encomiums of
Eva with an air of feigned indifference as she coldly
pressed her lips on its forehead and seemed to hurry it
from the room. Eva found the husband as she expected, full of ideas of self-importance; a thorough
specimen of a class of whom there fortunately are not
many; one who had imitated his mother by hanging
on the heels of people of fashion; who prided himself
on the superb beauty of his wife; and who, moreover,
ruled his household with a rod of iron.

Eva's visit was intended only for a few hours; she
endeavoured to persuade Dora to spend a short time at
Loskintyre, but in vain, and when left to themselves a
short time before their parting, Eva hazarded the question, affecting not to believe that Dora had really left
the Church, she received the following tart reply :—

"I belong, as does my husband, to the Protestant Church; I pray you, Eva, if we are ever to meet again, do not distress yourself on my account, I am perfectly happy."

Thus repelled, poor Eva held her peace, silent, but not convinced, especially as just then the husband approached, accompanied by a Presbyterian divine with whom they appeared to be on intimate terms; and unconscious that the lady whom Dora introduced as her sister, was a Catholic, launched out in no very favorable terms respecting the Church of Rome.

Dora's pale face wore, for a moment, a contemptuous sneer, as she exclaimed, "I pray you cease, Mr. Murray, my sister is a Catholic, I would wish this conversation changed;" and as the minister attempted to stammer forth some words which he meant as an apology, the sneer died away, and Eva saw that a tear had gathered in Dora's dark eye, and the countenance usually impassable in its coldness; the exquisitely cut features, so true a type of feminine loveliness, grew sad, and Eva felt that the canker-worm had long gnawed at the heart of this unhappy woman.

And when night advanced and Eva, consenting to remain at Strathburne till the morrow, had withdrawn to the elegant chamber prepared for her reception, she gazed out on the wide expanse of country around. There, in the soft moonlight which bathed the face of nature in its silvery light, lay the beautiful estate

which one, who evidently was a tyrant husband, had
possessed gold enough to purchase; yonder rose the
cliffs frowning down in grand sublimity on the quiet
vale beneath; within the apartment everything spoke
of opulence and luxury, and musingly Eva's thoughts
came back to far off days, to her mother's ill-starred
nuptials, to the wretched home of her youth, the evictions at Rossmore, her imbecile grandfather, the utter
abandonment of the worthless Morden, her sisters temporary and most strange home in the S—— Poor-house,
wherein the first seeds of future error were sown in the
mind of Dora; then, as she gazed around that handsome apartment and thought of her own sunny home
at Loskintyre, she mused over the strange and marvel-
lous dispensation of events which had so changed the
current of affairs, and along with these thoughts was
ever present to her mind's eye the face of the gentle
Catherine pursuing the quiet even tenor of her way, by
which she was so well preparing for eternity.

Sad at heart, Eva bade Dora farewell on the morrow, leaving her with the painful reflection that the
heart of the mistress of Strathburne was ill at ease
under the guise of outward show.

Some six weeks had passed after Eva's departure,
and October waned towards its close, amid storms
seldom known at the close of the Autumn season, the
evening had closed in unusually early, and Dora had
some time stood mournfully gazing on the opposite

cliffs veiled in the blue mist which enveloped them and noting the sere and withered leaves which fell in circling eddies in the path beneath the open window at which she stood.

Her liege Lord was absent for a few days on a visit to a neighbouring Laird prior to his return to England, and Dora beheld advancing towards the house a tall slender youth in whom she recognised a strange resemblance to Eva and Catherine, and also a dignified Ecclesiastic clad in the garb of the Catholic Priest. An irrepressible sensation, partly of pleasure, more than half of pain, shot across Dora's heart as she prepared to receive the strangers; why had they intruded on her? and her eyes fell beneath the keen glance of the Priest whom she now confronted. He was a stranger to her, she was utterly unknown to the Rev. Father Hubert, whose card she held in her hand; but her eyes are now rivetted on the young companion who introduces himself as her cousin, Bernard Fitzgerald, and Dora acknowledges the likeness of feature to that of her own family, and which had first attracted her attention. He then related how he was favored by being chosen the companion of the English Monk in his Scottish tour; how he had heard of his cousin Dora dwelling for a short time at Strathburne, and his pleasure at meeting with her; then, too, the young aspirant for Holy Orders spoke of his studies, of the much longed for time now rapidly approaching which should confer upon

him the minor orders and raise him to the rank of sub-
deacon, and whilst he spoke with so holy an ardour,
and blessed the providence of God, and the piety of his
aged grand-sire who had suffered so much persecution
sooner than see him cross the threshold of the Mission-
schools,—then Dora listened as one who heard not.
With her eyes fixed on vacancy she mused over the
past, wishing for the absence of her unbidden guests,
to whom, in the name of hospitality, as well as owning
the ties of kindred, she was obliged so unwillingly to
offer shelter for the night.

Then in the few hours that intervened after refresh-
ment was offered to her guests, came the disclosure,
the explanation which Dora had from the first moment
dreaded, and yet had felt must be made.

The choicest gifts both of nature and of grace had
been liberally bestowed on Father Hubert.   Himself a
convert, and springing from a family both high in rank
as well as wealthy, yet, the noble mind of the good
Monk had scorned them all, and turning from these
perishable advantages, consecrated himself to the service of God, and the salvation of souls.   Equally at
home with the learned and the simple, Father Hubert
was sought after by all who knew him ; and whilst the
Savan could pass many a happy hour, and oftentimes
add to the store he had already laid up in his own
mind, the less gifted and talented felt themselves
equally at ease in his company.   His figure was tall

and commanding, his complexion dark, his features regular and good; the lines about the mouth betraying the indomitable will of a Loyola, the fine forehead betokening the intellect with which he was endowed; in fine, Father Hubert was one of those master spirits whom God never fails to raise up in his Church, more especially at those times when she is peculiarly assailed by temptation, if a soul could be gained to the fold of Christ, and to this work more particularly did the good Monk seem called; not only did his fervid impassioned eloquence, for he was one of the finest orators, and his profound piety win many a heart, but even more powerful than all this was the few moments spent in private conversation, and if with strong and cultivated minds this master spirit was wont to appeal but rarely without avail, as his daily increasing convert friends could show, what wonder that the frivolous and weak Dora felt so overpowering a restraint creep over her, that her eye fell beneath his piercing glance, that she wished, and ardently desired, yet lacked the power to break her gilded fetters for which she had cast aside her faith.

It was true, as she surmised, that the Monk knew she had once bore the name of Catholic, and his visit had not been made without an end; and when he drew forth the unpleasant truth from her hesitating lips, when he strove to sound the depths of her heart, a

something, for which she could not at the moment account, restrained her, so that in the presence of this
noble soul, whom she had heard long years since, had,
whilst yet a youth, laid honors and wealth and dignities
at the foot of the Cross, like another Xavier, she shrunk
from owning herself so abject a thing as to have flung
aside the inheritance of the faith for lucre's sake, she
could not look without shrinking, in the calm earnest
countenance of the Monk, but like a guilty thing, she
cowered beneath his gaze, answered him with averted
eyes, and ever and anon watched narrowly the hand
of the time-piece, wishful that the power were hers
to break up the conversation, then to his mild per-
suasive words, as he set forth to her the value of
the treasure she had cast away, and asked, had
she known true peace of mind since, then Dora murmured forth the words, " My husband, I dare not, what
would he . . . . "

" *What doth it profit a man to gain the whole world
and lose his own soul*," replied the Monk; and as he
spoke his eyes glanced from the richly furnished apartment out on the open country beyond, where cliff and
glen and wood and water lay bathed in the clear moonlight; " bethink thee, my child, that a short time hence
and all these things will pass away and you will pass
with them; you have owned that since the days of your
youth you have not spoken to a Priest, will you not

grant me the sweet happiness of thinking that with
God's blessing I have had some share in bringing you
back to the fold from which you have strayed."

"God knows how I would wish," said Dora, her
generally calm and proud face now bathed in tears,
"God knows how I would wish to retrace the past;" for
a moment she paused as if communing with herself,
and the Monk beheld the tears trickle one by one
through the delicate hand with which she shaded her
face; then, as if ashamed of the unwonted emotion she
had betrayed, the haughty spirit obtained the mastery;
she passionately dashed the tears aside, her countenance, almost rigid in its beauty, assumed its ordinary
expression, and she exclaimed with earnest vehemence—

"I cannot, dare not thwart my husband's will; as
a Protestant he wedded me, and such I *must* and *will*
remain."

The moment of grace had assuredly passed, for such
a moment *had* been given to Dora; time and eternity,
they were hers to choose from; she had selected the
former, and now showing her eager desire to close the
conversation, she, herself, turned it to another topic.

Father Hubert saw that it would be in vain to attempt to renew it, and on the following morning when
he bade her farewell, he drew forth a small silver
crucifix of which he begged her acceptance, with the
promise that she would in future wear it.

And Father Hubert and her cousin Bernard departed,

and with a wistful gaze Dora watched their retreating
forms till a bend in the road hid them from her sight.
She then turned to her accustomed employment, but her
heart was not at ease; the pale ascetic countenance of
the Monk, and his earnest reproachful eyes fixed upon
her own, were ever present to her; the words "*What
will it profit,*" &c. seemed ever ringing in her ears; the
customary cloud which hung over her like a funeral pall,
pressed upon her heavier than ever since his visit,
which she termed ill-starred; a deep despondency settled on her spirits, which she could not shake off, save
when in her husband's presence or with company
around her; a forced and assumed gaiety usurped its
place; then with solitude came a reaction, and stealthily
drawing forth the crucifix which she secretly wore
around her neck, she would gaze reverently upon the
sacred symbol and muse upon the past, then weigh
well her chances of worldly weal or woe, and decide that
if even eternity were lost, time must be still her own.

Time passed on and Mr. Bennett still delayed to return to London; he had become acquainted with a
party of Englishmen making the tour of the Highlands,
bons vivants like himself, and thus it was that Autumn
had given place to winter, and still he lingered at
Strathburne.

It was one Sabbath morning, the air sharp and frosty,
and the snow had already began to fall, when Dora
wrapping herself up in a large furred mantle went into

the nursery, and with a manifestation of fondness kissed each of her children ere she left home against the desire of her husband, who, urging the severity of the weather, begged her at least not to go to the parish Church on foot; at least, he added, go no further than to the Presbyterian Kirk; and I, less courageous than yourself, will read my bible at home.

With this injunction Dora left home *never* to return.

The day passed on, anxiety was succeeded by fear, then by certainty, that some accident must have befallen her; but ere the early winter afternoon shaded all things in obscurity, servants were dismissed in all quarters to see if they could discover what had happened.

Neither in the Kirk, however, nor in Episcopalian Church, had Dora prayed that day; but, more than the length of a mile beyond either temple, small footsteps were found in the snow, which had fallen heavily since she had left her home; these footsteps were closely followed by her now agitated husband and his anxious servants, and they brought them to the ruins of what had once been a beautiful Gothic Church, dedicated in olden times to Saint Kilda; the roof was gone, the walls alone remained, showing in the elegant pinnacles and tracery, how delicate and beautiful that ruined temple must once have been. Here still lay the arm of a cross, there yet remained the credence table, a portion of the heavy stonework once yclept a font, the stone

slab, once the altar; and the cold wintry wind swept
with a mournful wail through the open apertures once
filled with stained glass.

One glance showed Mr. Bennett that this place was
empty, and he was turning in disappointment from the
spot, when he observed something glistening on the
broken slab of the ruined altar, which he instantly
recognised as having seen in the possession of his wife,
whom he had rallied on having, what he termed, a relic
of her former Papist practices.

It was the silver crucifix which Father Hubert had
given her, and the black ribbon to which it was
attached was still wet with the traces of recent tears;
away then they turned from the ruins of St. Kilda, and
still followed the small trace which they yet perceived,
and which was momentarily becoming more indistinct, for
the shades of evening were quickly advancing, and a fresh
fall of snow was rapidly filling up the very imperfect guide
left to them, and which now wound around the edge of
a deep and fearful precipice, the sides forming a steep
and jagged rock, the base washed by the waters of the
ocean, the waves of which beat against it with a sullen
monotonous roar. Now gasping for fear, for a hideous
apprehension had fastened on the hearts of all, they
crept around that narrow path, still discerning the
small trace which told them that Dora's steps had
turned to the summit of that fearful cliff: suddenly the
trace was lost, and in horror too deep for utterance, the

husband on bended knees leant as far as with safety to himself he dared to do over the dizzy height, and there beneath, suspended between the waters of the ocean and the deep blue sky, lay the mangled body of the hapless Dora; the dark hue of her richly furred velvet mantle strikingly conspicuous amidst the snow which lay like a white pall around her. Till the tide was fairly out, none dared venture to rescue the remains of the unhappy woman; but many hours later, when it was considered safe to make the attempt, a knot of men made their way to the spot, and removed the poor mangled body to Strathburne; and a few days later, amidst much pomp, the remains of the deceased wife of the citizen prince were borne to their last resting-place.

But people *would* talk: at first some entertained the idea that Dora had been robbed and murdered, but this was but the supposition of a moment, for her watch and purse were found upon her person, and only the traces of her own footsteps had been discovered; and to avoid attributing to her the guilt of suicide, it was then sug-- gested that strange as the idea appeared, it was *just* possible that she might have taken it into her head to walk, ere she proceeded to Church; had first visited St. Kilda's ruined Chapel, and then ventured up the dangerous ascent to which we have alluded, and from which advancing too near to the edge, she had probably missed her footing and was thus dashed to pieces against the rocks below: thus then it was that a verdict of

accidental death was returned; and gradually, when
Mr. Bennett in the course of a short time had left the
neighbourhood, the affair of Dora's death, with many
other events daily passing around us equally dreadful,
passed from the minds of the inhabitants of the place.

But there was another opinion, however, which filled
the minds of many, and amongst these her own
husband; the deep dejection of many previous months,
her evidently assumed gaiety, all rushed upon the minds
of her friends; the farewell embrace she had taken, on
that fatal morning, of her children, a visit which Dora
had not previously made on similar occasions; then her
journey, not to the Church, but to the ruined Chapel,
the terrible walk beside the cliff, with wintry winds
howling around her, and the pitiless driving snow-storm
beating in her face, and her mangled remains at the
base of the rock below, carried quite another interpre-
tation to the aching hearts of those who knew her best.

Her husband, Eva, and Catherine, knew full well,
as clearly as if they had seen her hurl herself from the
cliff, that the act was her own; that probably remorse
had preyed powerfully on her weak and ill-regulated
mind, and had prompted the fearful deed, which was,
too evidently, the unhappy Dora's suicidal act.

CHAPTER XX.

A voice from the crowd, several sharp *hits* are made, all of
which fail to *hit* the Rector's fancy.—The Rev. Gentleman's
drawing-room is turned for the nonce into a species of bear
garden.

IT was drawing towards the close of winter, nearly
three years following the evictions perpetrated by the
worthy Rector, that a small supper-party had assembled
together in the Rectory; the weather, though it drew
towards the end of February, was sharp and frosty, and
the occasional sighing of the wind as it swept through
the leafless branches of the trees, and the snow which
still lay thickly without enhanced the sense of home
comforts. Miss Deborah had drawn aside the heavy
curtains of crimson satin damask, and shuddering as
she gazed out on the clear cold night, turned with a
very delicious sense and appreciation of the blessings
she enjoyed, to survey the warm well-furnished room in
which she stood, filled with well-dressed and fashionable

people : the blaze of light from the lamps around, the ruddy gleam from the ample and highly.polished stove, richly cut decanters, filled with sparkling wine from the choicest vintages, and cheerful and happy faces, formed no unpleasing contrast to the natural dreariness of winter scenery.

The merriment of the company was at its height, and each person present was ready with some racy anecdote to add to the general amusement, when Miss Deborah said,—

"I am sure you will all allow, from the experience of your lives, that fact is more astounding than fiction ; I have heard what has much astonished me ; do any of you remember an old farmer of the name of Fitzgerald, whom papa was so unjustly calumniated, even by our true Protestant press, for evicting, with other turbulent Papists, some three years since ?"

Some few present signified their assent, and Deborah continued :

"Well, then, I can tell you what has become of his three grand-daughters ; they had the name of being very handsome, though *I* could never discover a pretty feature in the countenance of either of them : one of them has taken the veil, a year since, a rich lady paid her pension, in one of those abodes of bigotry and superstition which ought not to be suffered to exist in our enlightened age ; for I am at a loss to find what use there can be in a woman, who runs away from her duties, to shut herself up within four stone walls? and ——"

"It would be well for you, Miss Deborah, if you were one quarter as useful to society," exclaimed a voice, which seemed to come from the further extremity of the room; in which four old ladies, seated around a table, were gravely narrating the gaieties and follies of their youth; little heeding the more noisy and youthful coteries beyond, amidst whom were the Curate Tomkins and the Hon. Mr. Bishop.

"I am astonished, Mrs. O'Donnell, that you should speak to Deborah in such a way;" said the Rector, in an angry voice, and approaching the old lady in question, he added, "I thought you one of the pillars of our venerable Church, by law established, and am much surprised you can praise in any way the doings of the Papist."

The old lady, in unfeigned surprise, stammered out,—

"*I* praise Popish Convents, Mr. Bishop? *I* say anything to affront dear Miss Deborah? what *can* you be thinking of? I declare to you I have said not one word about her."

Much offended, however, the Rector strode away, nothing doubting but that his *soi disant* old friend had uttered a gross untruth; the squeaking treble voice was Mrs. O'Donnell's, she had lost all her teeth, and not a soul in the room articulated with such difficulty as did this venerable lady.

As to Miss Deborah, she had bridled up, became very red, and felt very angry; but her friends hastened to pacify her, excusing the old lady on the ground of her age and imbecility of mind; one of them, an old friend of ours, in the shape of our gallant Colonel Monteith, adding: "I should not much wonder if any of those Popish Priests get hold of her, if she dies a Papist yet; if this is the way she forgets herself—— But do go on with your story, dear Miss Deborah, what of the other two sisters?"

"Well, then, you remember, many of you, the second sister, Dora, who, if the three sisters really had any pretensions to prettiness, was certainly the best looking; well, she was introduced into good society by that very foolish but well meaning English friend of ours, Mrs. Bennett, and nicely she repaid her kindness in taking her out of a workhouse, for she stole, as many of you know, clandestinely, into the family of her benefactress, became Mrs. Edward Bennett, has been surrounded by every luxury the world can bestow, but has just come to a very shocking end, by accidentally falling off from the summit of a fearful cliff near her husband's estate; but the beauty of it is, that these wretched papists, her relatives, and others who knew her at Rossmore as well as in Scotland, affirm that it was no accident by which Dora met her end, but that she made away with herself in a fit of despair and remorse for having thrown off her Popish faith. They say that one night the grandson of old Fitzgerald, the very youth whom the besotted old man would not allow to attend our Mission Schools, and who is now preparing to be one of their Romish Priests, called on her in her husband's absence along with a Monk, one of those unhappy perverts whom we remember as simple Walter Hubert; that after their departure she grew daily more dejected, left home one Sabbath morning to go to Church, as her husband and servants thought; but she never did go there at all, but in the ruins of an old mass-house they found a silver crucifix which it is supposed this Monk or her cousin had given to her, and then in a storm of wind and snow, had climbed up that fearful cliff and thrown herself off. The verdict has been brought in accidental death. Of course every one knows this has merely been done to spare the feelings of her family; but however, her own friends have not kept their surmises to themselves, and as usual with the Papists, who always find out that our converts are not sincere, they do not scruple to say that Dora never was a sincere Protestant; and, but for fear of her husband, would have soon returned to her Church."

"Most beautiful and wretched of women," said the deep voice of the curate, "it is all too true; rest assured, Miss Deborah, than when these Roman Catholics become Protestants it is merely from motives of interest, or out of some spirit of temporary vexation; there is so much that they have all their lives held sacred; then to *disbelieve* that, I think there is not one in a thousand of them sincere."

" Mr. Tomkins, Mr. Tomkins, do you know *what* you are saying, have you lost your senses, man ?" said the Rector, levelling at him various furious glances, " you shall never officiate again in this parish, unless, before the present company, you retract every word that you have uttered."

" I know not what you mean, Mr. Bishop," said the poor little man, rising up, and growing between fear and anger combined, as white as the neck-cloth he wore, " I know not what you mean; I assure you it was never I who expressed such sentiments as those I have just heard pronounced in this Protestant assembly; where is the use of our Mission Schools and our Bible Societies, and our Scripture Readers," he added, stretching out his hands as he spoke; " if this be true, where is the use of the money we spend to help these benighted souls; where the use of the gold sent out to preach the Gospel to the Irish; where—

" Aye, where indeed ?" said the Rector's son, " it is really all thrown away; I begin to think it is very wrong for us to interfere with them; we are only doing harm instead of good."

" For shame, William," exclaimed both father and sisters in one breath, and exclamations of astonishment and surprise burst forth from every part of the room, the females still lending an eager ear to Deborah, who, amidst the general hubbub that prevailed, continued to tell them how much more fortunate those vulgar Fitzgeralds had been than they had any right to expect; for who or what were *they*, forsooth; and now she had that day heard that Miss Eva had been married these three years to a rich gentleman of large landed property both in Scotland and England; what could he see in her but poverty and low birth?

" He saw very *much* more," said a voice from among the crowd of gentlemen who were almost disposed to quarrel over the dispute which had taken place; " he saw respectability and virtue and intelligence, for money he cared not, and high birth he did not seek, and Eva is now both rich and happy, which doubtless Miss Deborah is very *glad* to hear."

There was now a general tumult in the room; Miss Deborah and her sister shed tears of vexation, which were called hysterics; the gentlemen waxed wrath in word and action; the Rector and the Curate were both excited, the former declaring that some disaffected persons were in the room who had dishonorably obtruded themselves in the orthodox society of his true friends, yet he knew not on whom to fix, and, as on a former occasion, decided on breaking up the party immediately, resolving, for the time to come, almost to determine to mix no more in company; certainly to invite no more large assemblies of persons as on the present occasion.

Little, however, deemed the Rector and his family

that Colonel Monteith, whom they knew not to have
been long a convert to the Catholic faith, had been the
firebrand which had thus excited the feelings of the
company; little did they think that when they bade
him farewell and told him they were so glad to see him
back in Ireland, that *he* was the man who had committed the sad crime of wedding poor Eva, or that ere
a week was over they would have the annoyance of
knowing that the Scottish Colonel was now in the
bosom of the Church Catholic; indeed, we have it on
record, that when this astounding intelligence became
really known, that Miss Deborah no longer *affected* a
fit of hysterics, but really had one, and was then taken
so alarmingly ill that she was not seen in public for
many weeks; for the fact was Miss Deborah had tried
to fancy the Colonel was a shining light of the reformed
Church, and would sooner or later yield himself a slave
to her charms, and end by leading her to the altar.

Reader, we wish we could say that in any way this
honorable and worthy Rector had amended or made
reparation for the evil he has done to Catholic society,
for the hearts he has broken, the hearths he has laid
waste, and the happiness he has destroyed, but such
is not the case; in this, our day, the Honorable and
Rev. Mr. Bishop, and many many others of his class
with whom poor Ireland is visited, no doubt for her
greater purification, still go on rampant in their wicked-
ness, but not always shall the wicked triumph; the day

of retribution will at length arrive, the Church shall still flourish amid ages of persecution, and God's supernal justice shall at last descend on the authors of so much misery, if not in this world, in that which is to come.

CHAPTER XXI.

Recognition.—Morden's repentance and death.

On a fair soft evening in the Spring of the same year, two religious ladies, Sisters of Charity, threaded their way through the labyrinth of dirty courts and streets off Drury Lane. Even these abodes of poverty seemed less dreadful in the calm quiet sunlight of the fresh Spring evening, and the younger Nun, our old acquaintance, gentle Kate Fitzgerald, whispered:

"Even these dull dirty courts catch a few rays of the bright sunshine; how pleasant is this fresh air." As she thus spoke they reached a house which had something less of an appearance of squalid poverty about it than many of those in its vicinity, and the two Nuns who knew one of its occupants well, ascended three flights of stairs, the elder of the two rapping on the door of an attic chamber on the third story.

It was opened by an aged woman whose countenance

bespoke that she was of Irish origin; on a miserable truckle bed in the room lay extended a woman whose dissolution was evidently near at hand; her countenance though pinched and wasted and the small aquiline features sharpened by sickness and want, still bore the traces of former beauty. In the corner of the room sat a child some eight years of age, and ever and anon the words burst forth, "my child, what will become of my child, when I am gone?"

The elder Nun attempted to offer words of consolation, bidding her hope for the best, and telling her that every effort would be made, and was in fact being already made, to save the child from the fate with which it was threatened, viz. the workhouse, and thus the certainty of being brought up as an enemy to the religion of its mother, whom her husband had long time deserted; every effort was indeed now being put into requisition to save this unfortunate from the fate otherwise reserved for it, in common with thousands of other Catholic children whom the agents of proselytism are enabled through their parent's poverty to snatch from the bosom of the Church.

"Sure, Mother Agatha," said the worthy old woman who was tending her dying charge, "and I am after telling you a sad tale. Only last night a fine boy was brought here to be put in the school at Wandsworth. The school was opened by the Government, they say, for the children of soldiers who have been killed in

battle; or the *Patriotic Fund*, I am tould, they call it.
Well, the wretched mother of this little boy, and a fine
fellow he is, has been so unfortunate as to throw off
her faith, tempted in the midst of her great poverty by
the money offered her by some people in Dublin, and
so, alanna, she has got leave to send her poor child to
this Protestant school; but you see the little fellow is
ten years of age, and a fine clever boy he is too, and he
remembers that he has been used to go to Mass, and
knows his Catechism well; and sure but the poor boy is
heart broken at the thought of going to this school, and
sad and sorrowful the little fellow looks, and innocently
says, 'when I am fourteen I shall leave the school and
will remember all the Priest has told me, and shall go
to Mass again;' but sure, one knows well the poor child
will be more like to forget and abuse our holy faith
than profess it."

"Yes, it was too true; this wretched child, a fine
intelligent boy, with his little heart yearning after the
practices of the faith in which he had been reared, was,
as many are by the apostacy of his own mother, won
over by English gold and English promises, thrown
amongst those who were adverse to his faith, which it
was a hundred chances to one but that he would lose
long before the time came for him to leave the school;
thus becoming either a bigotted Protestant, or sink into
the ranks of infidelity."

But to return from our digression: Mother Agatha

and our old friend Kate, were about to leave the house, when the poor woman earnestly begged that they would see a man who was lying dangerously ill in the adjoining room, and who having heard that the Sisters of Charity visited the sick, had begged to see them on their next calling at the house.

Accordingly they sought the stranger, whose room was far more miserable than that they had just quitted.

" Gaunt misery had indeed worn him to the bone;" aged before his time, his eyes large, dark, and piercing, were raised from their cavernous hollows into which they had sunk. The Sisters approached his miserable bed, and pushing back the long elf locks which strayed over his forehead, and raising himself by a strong effort, he supported himself on one elbow, and shading his face with the other hand, he gasped forth the words, " I am dying, starving and alone; yet I would not have sent for you had I known this. Speak! in mercy tell me are you Kate Fitzgerald?" Catherine involuntarily started as the tones of a voice but too well remembered struck upon her ear; yet surely, that haggard, miserable, wo-begone wretch, could not be the once handsome, fashionable Morden; Morden the spendthrift, the gambler, who had robbed herself and her sisters of their birthright; but it was all too true. Kate had lived in quietude and peace, and her features were unaltered; but the countenance of this man who had led a life of reckless crime, which in the end had plunged.

N

him into a state of positive destitution, whose days and
nights had been dedicated to the gratification of his
evil passions, had undergone so great a change that it
was no wonder that Kate knew him not till the tones
of his voice struck upon her ear.

Much shocked, she leaned over the miserable couch
and said; "You are quite right, I am Kate Fitzgerald,
and little thought to meet you here."

"Nay, curse me not Kate," the wretched creature
exclaimed, clasping his hands together; "foully, basely
have I injured you all; but I am and have long been
very miserable."

"Calm yourself," said Mother Agatha, "and we will
do all we can in extending the help you so sorely need;"
then she took some bread from the basket she carried
and a small bottle containing wine, and dipping the
bread therein she handed it to Morden, who devoured
it with ravenous voraciousness. After a few moments,
revived by the stimulating properties of the wine, he
said, again fixing his eyes on Kate,—

"I must tell you all, and then I shall feel calmer. I
had firmly resolved to do my duty by you all, but in
an evil hour I broke my resolution and returned to the
gaming table; I lost, and the stake had been a heavy
one; I tried again with no better success, returned
home miserable and unhappy, but determined to
return to my old haunt on the following night. Ill
fortune, however, pursued me still; one after another

became enriched at the expense of the innocent daughters of my late unhappy wife; and at length, stung to desperation by the heavy losses I had sustained, I staked more heavily than before. Again and again I lost; and at last ruined, undone, a beggar myself; and having beggared those whose inheritance I had purloined, I rushed from the gambling house, the scene of my guilt and misery, and with the few trifling pounds which I still had on my person, I left London for Paris, where I, after much difficulty, procured a little employment as teacher of languages.

" In course of time, however, my employer died, all my future efforts failed, and I resolved to return to London. I could, however, obtain no further employment; and as time went on my resources became more and more exhausted, till, long since, they failed altogether. I find myself on the brink of eternity in the prime of a wasted life, guilty in the extreme, for my soul has been steeped in almost every vice that can disgrace manhood. I have now to appear before the tribunal of offended heaven; I have it not in my power to make any restitution, but "—

" Do not afflict yourself on this account," said Kate, " I need not any portion of my deceased father's property. Eva is rich as to this world's goods, and poor Dora is no more."

A faint gleam of satisfaction passed across the wasted features of the wretched Morden as Kate spoke, and a

fervent " Heaven be thanked " escaped his lips, and
she beheld tears course over that emaciated face.

The lips of the Nuns moved not, but their hearts
were busily employed in fervent prayer that the moment of grace might not pass disregarded by, and after
the pause of a few moments the wretched Morden
exclaimed,—

" I know but little of God, or of the eternity to which
I am hastening; I pray you, Kate, bring to me some
good Priest of your Church who can teach a sinner
how to die."

" You shall see one ere the night has closed in,"
replied Mother Agatha; " we will now leave you and
will see you again early to-morrow; but before we go,
we will leave the means for affording you present nourishment with the good woman who asked us to call
upon you. Now farewell," she added, " keep your
mind easy, we will not forget you."

" Your forgiveness, my gentle Kate," murmured the
sorrow-stricken Morden, as she bade him farewell; " I
have deeply wronged you all; both your dead mother
and yourselves."

" Not a word more," said Kate, or sister Winifred,
as she was called in religion, turning away as she
spoke to conceal her tears, " I thank God who has
brought me to you," she added, " and hope to see you
better both in mind and body on the morrow."

But Morden never saw the rising of the morrow's

sun; the Priest whom the sisters sent remained with him, for he saw that the death agony was at hand. With sentiments of apparently the deepest contrition for the errors of so sadly mispent a life, the miserable Morden made his first and last confession, and on the bed of death was received into the Church, whose teachings he had in the days of health and strength despised. But little reliance can, unfortunately, be placed on death-bed repentances; but, as far as there was room to judge, there was every reason to believe that that of the too guilty Morden was at least sincere.

CHAPTER XXII.

In which the family of the Honorable and Rev. Rector appear
again upon the scene.—A liberal provision is offered; soup,
clothes, cottage, if Tim Murphy will but send his girls to
Miss Martha's school, and himself and wife forsake the
Minister of Anti-christ and follow the godly teaching of
Mr. Tomkins.—The author's farewell.

DEAR old Ireland, how heavily is visited on thy head
the sin of having preserved the inheritance of thy faith,
thy veneration for thy maligned and persecuted Clergy,
thy deep love of the Church of ages; that Church triumphant amidst her poverty, and never more glorious
than when most persecuted and reviled. Of a truth,
sons and daughters of Erin, is thy patience sorely
tried, when we think of the miserable handful of Scotch
Presbyterians burthened with no State Church, and
remember the multitudes in the Emerald Isle who bear
the time-honored name of Catholic, with the incubus of
the Established Church weighing heavily upon them,

then do we ourselves of half-English, half-Scotch extraction, in whose veins flows not a drop of Irish blood, marvel that poor Ireland has so patiently borne the grievances imposed on her by the Establishment with its *Glebe* and *See*, and *Trinity College Lands*, amounting, as certifies a recent Report, to no less than a total of 1,000,602 statute acres, exclusive of Charter and Royal School Lands, and in addition to the Tithe Rent Charge, amounting, yearly, to the sum of £360,000 per annum.

Ah! ye sons of stern John Knox, uncompromising Presbyterians, such a yoke has never galled *thy* stiff shoulders as that which presses so unjustly on the Catholics of Ireland.

But here we are on a cold March morning, some two to three years since the evictions took place, nothing daunted either by the wrathful spirit he has evoked in those dwelling in the immediate neighbourhood around Rossmore, by the misery his intolerance has caused, or by the expressions of indignation emanating from the public Press both in England and Ireland, even from the great Anti-Catholic organ, the daily *Times*, which called such conduct *a hideous scandal*, the Honorable and Rev. Rector pursues the path he has chalked out for himself and family to follow.

The morning of which we speak was, as we have said, bitterly cold, a cutting north-east wind blowing over the mountains of Rossmore; yet two ladies and a gentleman manfully brave the severity of the weather, for they are engaged on an errand of Evangelical zeal. Miss Deborah and her sister Martha are, in company with the Curate, wending their way to a poor and wretched home on what they deem a mission of charity. Outstripping her companions by reason of her long masculine strides, her never good tempered countenance now bearing a more unamiable expression than usual, she pursued her way in moody silence. Leaning on the arm of Mr. Tomkins, Miss Martha pursued the same path at a slower pace. More feminine in form and manner than her sister, by no means handsome yet far from ugly, less *brusque* than Miss Deborah, dividing her time between the Mission Schools and her bullocks, for Miss Martha is the farmer of her family and keeps cattle on her own account, she walked demurely by the side of Mr. Tomkins, a strong contrast to her companion, for Martha is, as we have said, very feminine, and her eyes have a most gentle expression in them. The Curate's forehead is drawn up into wrinkles, thus conveying the idea of his mind being *mal à son aise*, and that perpetual offensive grin hovering about the thin lip, is brought on by his constant practice of ridiculing Popery; which, with the restless expression about the whole *contour*, renders his countenance so unpleasing.

Down on the moors are scattered a few wretched huts, and to one of these the party turn their steps. Only dimly through the smoke issuing from a small peat fire can they at the first glance take in the interior of the hut in which they now stand; then, as their eyes become more accustomed to the obscurity of the place, they can discern a wretched half-clad, half-starved woman, her once handsome features sharpened by want. To her milkless breast she presses a miserable babe, whilst three elder children cower over the smouldering peat. "Is your husband at home, Mrs. Murphy," enquired Mr. Tomkins in his blandest tones. "We have heard that you are all in sore distress, and the Lord hath opened the hearts of the Misses Bishop; they have come here with me to-day, leaving their warm comfortable home to bring you aid, if you are prepared to profit by it.

"Sure, and the ladies are very good, Sir," replied the poor woman, dropping a curtsey as the spoke, "for my husband can scarce walk; but he has crept up to Father De Vere to ask his Riverence if he thinks the rich folk who are coming to live at the fine house, down the other side of Rossmore, will give us a wee bit or sup, for it is after starving we are, and if the ladies would help us a little, sure and we'll pray to the good God for them as long as we live."

"Yes, yes, I do not doubt you," replied Mr. Tomkins, and the odious grin we have spoken of increased as he added, "Now, Mrs. Murphy, I have a proposal to make to you on the part of these good ladies; you know the pretty cottage on the moors beyond, which is now empty; well," he continued, as the woman nodded assent, "this, Miss Bishop will give your husband with the piece of land around it, and Miss Martha will give you a couple of pigs and warm clothing for yourself and children with a small sum of money, if you will consent to abandon the teaching of the Minister of Antichrist, leave the Mass-house for ever, and send these poor children whom you are bringing up in so much superstition to our Mission Schools."

For one instant, it might be, the mind of that poor creature wavered; food and raiment and a comfortable home on the one side, destitution and starvation, perhaps, on the other. She glanced at her almost dying babe, she looked at her pale and famished children, and the tear sparkled in her eye, as in a tone of deep feeling she then exclaimed—

"Whist, Sir, but if it is after tempting us again you are, I may not listen to you; 'Lead us not into temptation,' she added, reverently crossing herself as she spoke, "Sure, and does not his Riverence, Father De Vere, teach us how to be good and patient; and though we are often after thinking God tries us so much, sure, Sir, the passion and death of Christ was more than this."

"Poor woman, from my soul I pity you," exclaimed

Miss Deborah, "for the Lord hath mercifully opened our hearts to come to your aid and you refuse, and love the darkness better than the light."

"Well said, Kathleen, agra," exclaimed a voice, and a man, bearing on his whole person marks of the severest penury now entered the hut. "Now, ladies," he added, "you know that once I *did* send my children to the Mission Schools, but sure it was against my conscience, and I could not rest till I removed the wee things again, and it is after telling us you are, that you will only help us if we go amongst the Jumpers, and will leave us to starve if we serve God as our conscience tells us we should do."

"My good man," replied the Curate, "you are buried in the errors of Popery; yet, again and again by *my* voice, has the Lord called you out of that sink of uncleanness."

"Have pity on your wretched children, Murphy, if not on yourselves," said Miss Martha, "and remember that we cannot throw the bread of the children to dogs; the Lord has made us stewards of His property, and we must not help those who wallow in the errors of Rome; but gladly will we help you, my poor people, if you will allow us to do so." As Miss Bishop spoke thus, she was attracted by sound such as would be caused by the rustling of silk, and raising her eyes, she beheld standing in the doorway of the hut, a lady of whose features she fancied she had an indistinct remembrance; yet, in common with her companions, she did not recognise in the veiled stranger, our old friend Eva, whom, indeed, they had only once met on the occasion of her visit to Mr. Bishop's residence at Laurel Hill, immediately before the evictions in the famous Rossmore case had taken place; especially as the slightness of the girl had given way to the maturity of womanhood.

Slightly bowing to the little party whom she well remembered, Eva entered the hut, exclaiming with a smile, (Ah! Eva, marriage has not sobered thee, thou wilt be always mischievous.) "I fear I am forestalled in my charitable intentions, and that *you*, ladies, have been the first in doing a good work; surely there is room for charity here," she murmured; and, advancing, she passed her hand caressingly over the cold pale face of the baby, which derived neither warmth or nourishment from the bosom on which it lay nestled.

"The Lord, Madam, has indeed opened the bowels of His charity," said the Curate Tomkins, in behalf of these poor people, "for he has graciously inspired these ladies to give them permanent relief and a peaceful happy home if they will but accept it."

"Accept it," replied Eva, in an accent of astonishment, glancing around the wretched poverty-stricken hut, and on the wan pale faces of its inmates, "surely these poor people would be mad to refuse succour if God be pleased to send it."

As Eva spoke thus the poor woman burst into tears, and replied, " Sure, my lady, and it is after starving we are; not a wee bit have we had since yesterday morning, but we cannot go amongst the Jumpers, or send our children to the Mission Schools, and unless we do, not a bit or sup will be given to us."

As the poor woman spoke thus her voice sunk into a low melancholy wail, and she rocked the whining babe to and fro on her milkless bosom.

" In the name of humanity," exclaimed Eva, proudly confronting the little party, " do not tell me that these wretched people speak the truth; yet, wherefore should I doubt," she added, somewhat satirically, " for I believe I address Mr. Tomkins and the Misses Bishop;" and she again bowed as Miss Deborah stared at her through the gold opera glass which that lady held in constant requisition, " I suppose the offers of help are backed by conditions such as Murphy and his wife, wretched as they are, cannot accept."

" They follow the Minister of Antichrist," said Tomkins, " and unless they renounce his teaching the Lord will leave them to perish in their idolatry."

" But the Lord has *not* deserted them, or left them to perish," exclaimed Eva, throwing aside the veil which had partially obscured her features; " remember you not, ladies, my grandsire, Bernard Fitzgerald, whom the intolerant spirit of your father drove to imbecility and death; am I quite forgotten at Rossmore, where,

thanks to God, as the wife of Colonel Monteith, I may
have it *somewhat* in my power to alleviate the suffering
you are still daily causing."

Mesdames Deborah and Martha stammered out a
few words of astonishment and virtuous indignation at
the remarks of Eva, the former stepping in longer
strides than usual around the hut, now made her way
across the moors, followed by her sister. The Curate
still lingered, venting his rage in sundry malignant
epithets against the Man of Sin, as he was pleased to
style Father De Vere, till Eva insisted on his leaving
her to the quiet performance of the charitable acts
which his intolerant spirit prevented him from exer-
cising.

Sweet, indeed, was the pleasure Eva experienced in
having it in her power to alleviate the sorrows she
beheld around her, her first act of charity being exercised in behalf of Murphy and his family, whom the
Colonel placed, a little later, in a comfortable farm on
his own estate of Fairview, of which he had but a day
or two previous become the master.

*   *   *   *   *   *   *

"And this estate is really ours," said Eva to her husband, and she surveyed with an air of gratified pleasure
a small but pretty and trimly kept domain, the
grounds of which adjoined those of the worthy Earl of
Rathmore.

"Yes," replied the Colonel, " I desire to have a home

of our own in Ireland; for the Emerald Isle, my Eva, is still your fatherland, and I would not wish the ties that connect you with it to be broken.

A few months, then, out of each year were designed to be spent in Ireland, thus keeping up the friendly relations which existed between herself and Father De Vere, and their intercourse with the good Lord Rathmore and his Countess; and we have it on record that the clerical dignitary who has not scrupled to send forth his emissaries with crow-bar and pick-axe, evinced no small annoyance on learning, that Colonel Monteith whom he had known when the former was a Protestant, had purchased the estate of Fairview, which was not very far from his own.

And now, dear reader, we have but little more to say; we would fain hope that your own hearts have sympathized in the various events we have recorded. Our picture is life-like; for, after all, imagination has had but little share in the above narration. You know how much the Catholic Priest has to endure in his visits to the pauper homes of the destitute, and how lately, a clerical personage in faithful old Ireland has acted like the Rector in our tale. Furthermore, we may add that the death of the hapless Dora is no fiction; the gambler Morden no unreal character, for such an one in truth existed, and through his vices his step-daughters, robbed of their birth-right, were plunged, as we have said into the horrors of a workhouse.

We have now then only to bid you adieu, dear reader; to beg you to be kindly indulgent, though, mayhap, were our talent less humble, we might in speaking of certain doings in dear and faithful old Ireland, have delineated them with a more powerful pen, or in more eloquent language.

Yet, we will trust that our tale of Eva may find grace with our friends in the Sister Isle, that criticism may deal gently with it, and that you, dear reader, may, notwithstanding its faults, peruse with interest these pages, is the wish of your humble servant,

THE AUTHOR.